Elsi

A Paperback Exchange
137 E. Pine St.
Cadillac, MI 49601
616-775-8171

"Call me Justin."

His eyes sparkled and his mouth threatened to smile.

She blushed. *This man certainly has a way of making me feel at a disadvantage.* She looked down at her notebook to escape his penetrating stare. *He's probably counting the wrinkles in my crow's feet.*

"Okay," he said, suddenly businesslike. "Penny can show you the files and our standard will, so I don't need to dictate all the first part, about revoking all other wills, et cetera, okay?"

She hoped it was okay. She hadn't done any wills while working for the district attorney in Colorado.

"Marino's wife died three years ago," Justin began. "Strange, too. She was only thirty-seven. Had some kind of heart disease. Anyway, he wants to update his will. Oh, and make a note. I want you to call my former partner. Penny can give you the number. Tell one of the secretaries over there that Marino is drawing up a new will with me. Just a courtesy so they don't have a lot of dead wood in their files."

He studied the document before him, which Suzanne assumed was a copy of Mr. Marino's old will. A good secretary didn't stare at her boss while he was gathering his thoughts, she knew, but she couldn't resist some quick peeks. He was a strange, yet almost beautiful man. He reminded her of Michelangelo's statue of David, except that he was so alive. The scent of his pleasant-smelling shaving lotion also reminded her of something, but she couldn't call it to mind.

The Book Nook
A Paperback Exchange
124 E. Pine St.
_____, MI 4____
(517) 773-8171

A NEW LOVE

Mab Graff Hoover

Serenade/Serenata BOOKS
of the Zondervan Publishing House
Grand Rapids, Michigan

A Note from the Author:
I love to hear from my readers! You may correspond with me by writing:

> Mab Graff Hoover
> 1415 Lake Drive, S.E.
> Grand Rapids, MI 49506

A NEW LOVE
Copyright © 1986 by The Zondervan Corporation
Grand Rapids, Michigan

Serenade/Serenata is an imprint of Zondervan Publishing House,
1415 Lake Drive, S.E., Grand Rapids, Michigan 49506.

ISBN 0-310-47212-1

All rights reserved. No part of this publication may be reproduced,
stored in a retrieval system, or transmitted in any form or by any
means—electronic, mechanical, photocopy, recording, or any
other—except for brief quotations in printed reviews, without the
prior permission of the publisher.

Edited by Anne Severance
Designed by Kim Koning

Printed in the United States of America

86 87 88 89 90 91 92 / 10 9 8 7 6 5 4 3 2 1

CHAPTER 1

SUZANNE FORREST STOOD AT THE THRESHOLD of Suite 206-209, in Hacienda Heights' newest, glass-walled office building. She was dressed in last year's Easter outfit, a sheer, navy blue two-piece dress with a white eyelet ruffle at the neck, and although it was a little snug around her waist, and too thin to wear this breezy March day, she looked as she hoped she would—pretty, dignified, and competent. Her shining brown hair swirled around her shoulders as she readjusted the strap of her bag and took a tremulous breath.

She needed this job. There would be no help from Del; his desertion of his family left her with full responsibility for the household. Of course she would have to have child support for Randy and the baby, at least until she could get established, but in her heart she didn't want anything from the man who no longer loved her.

Suzanne's hand was moist as she gripped the knob and turned it. Her neighbor, Selena Garcia, had told her about this job. "He's a young lawyer who's just opened an office right here in Hacienda Heights," she had said. "He'll have to have a secretary." Always involved in local politics, Selena had met the attorney in the mayor's office. "And he looks like a movie-star!" she had added, her brown eyes sparkling. "Who knows, maybe you two—" But Suzanne had cut her off. "All I'm interested in is a job." And so, she had made this appointment for an interview.

She glanced up at the brass nameplate and read, "Justin David Wheatley, Attorney at Law." She had been a legal secretary before she married Del, but it had been at least six years since she had taken shorthand. *Please, Lord. Don't let him give me a test.* With her lips slightly parted, she opened the door.

The reception room was larger than she anticipated, carpeted in blue, and furnished with light blue chairs and glass-topped wooden tables. Part of the room had been partitioned with waist-high paneling to form an office.

A young woman whose auburn hair curled around her shoulders and whose eyes were the color of a bluebird, sat at a desk behind the paneling. Suzanne felt a quick stab of disappointment. He had already hired a secretary.

"You must be Suzanne Forrest," the woman said smiling.

"Yes." Suzanne's mouth was dry when she tried to return the smile.

"Mr. Wheatley's expecting you, but he's with a client. He won't be long. Please sit down." She looked directly into Suzanne's eyes. "And don't worry. He's easy to talk to."

Suzanne laughed nervously. "I hope so!" She sat down in one of the new chairs and picked up a copy of *Time*. She flipped through it, but couldn't concentrate on any of the news items. Every few seconds she looked at the girl behind the desk. She was sorting papers into stacks, evidently getting ready to file

8

them. Finally, Suzanne had to make sure. "Are you Mr. Wheatley's secretary?"

She shook her head. "Heavens, no." Her voice had a happy lilt to it. Suzanne's shoulders relaxed. "I'm the receptionist. I barely know how to type." She giggled and hunched her shoulders. "By the way, my name's Penny Davidson."

"Hi." This time Suzanne found it easier to smile.

"He hasn't had a secretary since he moved into this suite about three weeks ago."

"Oh?" Suzanne raised her eyebrows and hoped Penny would tell her more.

"Mr. Wheatley used to be in a partnership over in Whittier, but he decided to go it alone. And, of course, the secretaries stayed with the senior partner." She flipped her hair back over her shoulders. "He hired me the first week, and he's interviewed several for the job . . ." She lifted her palms and shrugged. "But he hasn't hired anyone yet."

Suzanne swallowed. *He must be hard to please*, she thought. *But I cannot let myself be disappointed if he doesn't hire me. I'll get a job, somewhere.* She noticed another desk behind the partition, a shining desk, and a blue, deluxe steno chair. *Just waiting for me*, she thought wistfully. When she had worked for the district attorney in Arapahoe Country she had had a nice office. She had loved her job and didn't quit until the last few months of her pregnancy with Randy. *If he hires me, and I can take his dictation, I'm sure I'll be happy here, too*, she thought. *That is, as happy as a woman can be who's husband is divorcing her.*

There were some nice prints on the wall, Suzanne observed. To the right, a hall led from the waiting room down to an area she couldn't see from her chair. From that direction she heard a door open, then men's voices. Her heart began to thud.

"Thanks a lot, Justin," one man said. "You've eased my mind."

"Just bring in everything you can find on the subject," the other voice answered as they drew nearer, "and I'm sure we'll have a case."

Suzanne leaned forward slightly, eager to see Mr. Justin David Wheatley. Two men strolled from the hall and stood directly in front of her. Both were tall. Both wore suits. One man had almost black, wavy hair, parted on the side. The other, who appeared to be younger, had thick blond hair that waved back from a middle part. Suzanne bit her lip. Which one was Mr. Wheatley? Selena had said he was handsome, but both men were good-looking.

"If you think of anything else, Vincent, call me," the blond man said. *Ah,* Suzanne reasoned, *if the dark one is Vincent, then the blond one has to be Mr. Justin David Wheatley.*

"Will do, Justin," the dark man answered and put a big hand on the doorknob. He waved at Penny and went out.

Without a glance at Suzanne, the attorney went back down the hall. A door thudded. In a moment a buzzer sounded on the desk.

Penny picked up the phone, listened, then winked at Suzanne. "Yes, Mr. Wheatley," she said. When she had put the phone back, she stood and said, "He'll see you now." A slender Barbie-doll figure, Penny came out the little gate, and led the way down the short hall to Mr. Wheatley's office. On the way Suzanne noticed rest rooms on the left, and a supply room, with a Xerox machine, on the right.

Penny knocked lightly on the last door, then opened it. "Mrs. Forrest," she announced, and motioned for Suzanne to go in.

Mr. Wheatley was signing papers, and it seemed a long time before he finally looked up. She had time to notice the walnut furniture, a full, floor-to-ceiling bookcase, his framed diplomas, and some exceptional photographs of Yosemite. She wondered if he had taken them.

At last he put the pen back in the desk set and smiled up at her. "Sit down."

He was dressed in an expensive-looking tan suit, and Suzanne looked into eyes that were as green as her own when she placed her resume on his desk. She looked away quickly and sat in the leather chair across from his desk, her navy purse in her lap.

He glanced at the resume, then put it aside. "Just tell me what it says . . . a condensed version, please." His expression was friendly, although slightly sardonic. She struggled to be calm, and forced herself to look into his eyes.

"I'm married," she began, and immediately felt guilty for not admitting the full story. Yet, in the confusion of trying to adjust to the new status forced upon her, she had let Selena talk her into wearing her wedding rings. "That way you don't have so many creeps trying to set you up until you get your thoughts together," she had advised.

"—and I have two children," Suzanne continued. Justin Wheatley looked at her quickly, then reached for the resume. He studied it a moment.

"How old are you?" he asked, still scanning the page.

She hesitated, wondering if he would think she was too old. But her birthdate was on the resume anyway. Trying to sound indifferent, she answered, "Thirty-two."

He cocked his head and lifted an eyebrow as though surprised.

She cleared her throat. "I've had several jobs in the past. My last one was as a legal secretary."

He leaned back in the leather chair and locked his fingers across a flat stomach. "Tell me about that job."

She touched her tongue to her lips. "I worked in Colorado as secretary to the district attorney of Arapahoe Country for two years."

11

"Recently?"

She twisted the fastener on her purse. "A few years back."

He continued to stare at her, unblinking. At last he said, "Tell me about some of your duties. Did you have any outstanding cases?"

She smiled. "There wasn't an awful lot going on. But I took verbatim notes, at inquests—"

"Oh, really? Do you use a stenotype?"

"No, but my shorthand is very good."

"How's your typing?"

"Seventy. And I'm accurate and neat."

"What legal experience have you had in California?"

She felt defeated. Goodbye job, probably, if she couldn't produce any local references. She lifted her chin. "None," she said distinctly. "But I'm positive I can do your work." His eyes tried to stare her down, but she smiled and looked straight into his. "I'm a quick study."

He smiled, almost imperceptibly, then swung around in his chair, with his back to her. He stared out the window, which overlooked the Pomona freeway. The room was so quiet Suzanne could hear herself swallow. *Dear Lord, You know I need this job*.

After a moment, he turned his chair back around and asked, "Can you verify what you've just told me?"

"Of course."

"How much salary do you expect?"

"Salary?" she stalled.

Suzanne had discussed this with both Selena and Harriet, her mother-in-law. Both of them advised her to ask for what seemed an enormous amount.

"Listen," Selena had urged. "People make more dinero now than when you were working. Didn't you ever hear of inflation?" Suzanne had finally called the Bureau of Labor Statistics and they gave her a starting figure, which still seemed too high.

12

When she hesitated, Wheatley frowned at her. She met his eyes, and although she trembled inside she stated the amount boldly.

"Sounds fair," he said and picked up her resume once more. "Suzanne Forrest. Anyone call you Susie?"

"Every now and then."

"Do you mind?"

She smiled. "A rose by any other name smells as sweet."

He chuckled. "Can you start tomorrow?"

She drew in her breath. "What time?"

"Eight-thirty." He stood up, looked down at her and pointed an index finger. "Not eight-thirty-five. Eight-thirty."

She nodded. "Fine. I'll be here." He came around the desk and held out his hand, and as he pulled her to her feet she felt flushed and breathless. At that moment she made up her mind to get back in shape; she hadn't lost all the weight she gained before she had Crystal. He opened the door. "We'll see you in the morning, then."

As she walked down the hall, conscious of his gaze, he called softly.

"By the way, Susie, there may be some night work."

CHAPTER 2

SOME NIGHT WORK. SUZANNE MUSED, as she unlocked her old Toyota station wagon. She got behind the wheel, a puzzled expression on her face. What did that mean? Her eyes narrowed as she started the engine. Wonder what Selena would make of it?

She backed out of the space and drove slowly out of the parking lot. "Oh!" she said under her breath. "I know what Selena will make of it." She raised her eyebrows, and shook her head, imitating her fiery Mexican-American neighbor, "Well what do you think night work means, babee?"

Why had she been so stupid when he tossed that at her? She had turned around, smiled, and said, "Whatever." No questions. Like a lamb to slaughter. "But I couldn't take a chance on losing the job," she defended out loud. "And it's probably perfectly innocent." A man standing on the corner stared at her as she waited for the light to change. Suppressing a smile, she looked away. *He probably thinks I've lost my mind, sitting here, with no one else in the car, talking my head off.*

She drew in a deep breath and let it out. Her shoulders sagged, and she realized how tense she had been. She glanced back at the new building where she would be working, and smiled. *At least I got the job. If he does try anything, I'll set him straight. But the main thing is, I got the job. Thank the Lord.*

By the time she turned into her driveway she was whistling softly, an unconscious act which wasn't exactly whistling, but a tuneless whooshing of breath through her pursed lips. It was an expression of happiness she had adopted as a little girl. When she turned off the key and could hear herself, the wheezy sound startled her. It'd been a long time since she had 'whistled.' When she had learned that it drove Del crazy to hear it, she had finally learned not to do it in front of him, and had gradually quit it altogether. But she felt so happy right now! *You've come a long way,* she said to herself.

She unlocked the front door and hurried toward the kitchen, eager to tell Harriet about the interview. Her mother-in-law was a good friend. She had made herself available, both for comforting and baby-sitting since Christmas night when Del had told her he was leaving her for someone else, and walked out.

"Hi!" Suzanne called. "Good news!" Harriet was feeding Crystal in the highchair, and when she turned around to greet Suzanne, the baby clasped chubby hands around her yellow dish and threw it as far as she could. The dish hit the floor at Suzanne's feet, and the soft food splattered Suzanne's shoes and skirt. Crystal squealed with pleasure.

"Crystal!" Suzanne scolded, her brows scowling. "Look what you did. Bad girl! You've ruined my dress!"

Harriet stood, grabbed a tea towel and began to wipe Suzanne's skirt. "I don't believe it's ruined, dear," she said softly.

As Suzanne looked down at her mother-in-law's

short, salt and pepper hair, she wilted with shame. "Oh, Harriet, I'm so sorry." She turned to Crystal and saw her blue eyes were wide and frightened. The red lips had squeezed to a tiny circle, then suddenly opened wide in a loud wail. Gigantic tears popped out of her eyes and rolled down her cheeks.

Suzanne spoke more softly. "Oh, baby, Mommy's sorry." She sank down in a chair and closed her eyes. Harriet stood and walked over to lift Crystal from the high chair, trying to soothe her. She had been so happy a few minutes ago. Why had Crystal made her so furious? Didn't all babies throw their food? But she had spanked Crystal for that before, and felt she knew better. Was she going to be a stubborn child?

"I don't know what I'm going to do with her, Harriet," she said huskily.

"Oh, Sue, she's perfectly normal." Harriet said, sitting beside her with Crystal. "She's just a little spoiled, that's all."

Suzanne bit her tongue not to make known who the chief spoiler was. Harriet had been wonderful and supportive since Del left—coming over almost every-day to help her, offering a free baby-sitting service, yet she always brought little treats to the children and let them have their way in almost every instance. Now, both of them acted like little moochers.

Harriet didn't seem to notice Suzanne's silence. She made a funny face to make the baby smile, then began to chant, "Patta-cake, patta-cake, baker's man . . ." Crystal began to pat her chubby hands together. Harriet laughed and cooed, "Her just has to get her way, doesn't her?"

Suzanne jumped to her feet impatiently and walked to the refrigerator. That was another thing that was pulling on her already taut nerves—baby talk. "Did Randy eat okay?"

"I should say. Two hot dogs, buns, jello, milk—"

Suzanne cut in. "Oh, I got the job."

"—some cookies." Harriet looked at Suzanne. "You got the job? Honey! I thought . . . I mean, the way . . . you seemed so upset."

"I know. I was so happy I got the job, but Crystal's temperament does affect me."

"Well, she's just a little bit . . ."

Suzanne shot Harriet a look as she opened the refrigerator.

Harriet swallowed, then spoke pleasantly. "Tell me about the interview."

Suzanne took out a package of cheddar cheese and slashed at the tough plastic with a paring knife. She sliced a piece of cheese and ate it without really tasting it. She poured a cup of coffee, then sat down at the kitchen table. Harriet's brown eyes were sympathetic, and she was leaning forward expectantly. Her mother-in-law had made a lot of sacrifices for her, and she must try and be more understanding. There were just so many changes to get used to. At last Suzanne felt calm enough to start talking.

"He was really nice, Harriet. I felt scared, sort of." She brightened. "But, you know something? You and Selena were right about the money." Her eyes crinkled at the corners as she told what her salary would be, and she could feel her usual good humor returning. "When I told him the amount I expected, he didn't hesitate."

"Good! And you're worth every penny. When do you start?"

Suzanne groaned. "Tomorrow!" She bit her lip. "Can you keep the kids?"

After an almost imperceptible hesitation Harriet said, "Of course."

Had there been a shadow of weariness in Harriet's eyes, or had she imagined it? *Imagination or not*, she thought, *I won't impose on her any longer than I have to.* Aloud, she said, "It'll be only for the rest of this week, or maybe even less, if I can get someone. I'll put an ad in the Highlander."

"Well, we don't want just anybody for this precious thing." Harriet kissed Crystal's cheek and hugged her tightly.

"Grandma wouldn't think you were very precious this morning," Suzanne grumbled as she changed a messy diaper. "Why now, you tootsie-poo?" Suzanne glanced at her watch and gasped. "It's already eight-ten! Be still, Crystal! Mommy's got to be there on time."

"Suzanne?" Harriet called from the kitchen. "I just came on in."

"I'm glad you're here, Harriet," Suzanne yelled back. "Be right there."

In the kitchen she handed a clean and smiling Crystal to Harriet and said, "I'm sorry you had to walk down, but—"

"No, no. That's fine. I need the exercise."

"You mean you don't think you'll get enough chasing this kid today?" She leaned over and kissed the baby's neck. "I'll probably have to carry you out tonight."

"You know, Sue," Harriet tipped her head slightly and pursed her lips for a moment, "I've been thinking. Wouldn't it be easier for both of us if I stayed here?" Suzanne stared at Harriet, her mouth slightly open. Harriet went on. "I mean, just for a few days, until you get a real sitter."

"Oh." Suzanne cleared her throat. "Well. You're probably right." She picked up her purse, then smiled brightly. "We can talk about it tonight." She looked up at the kitchen clock. "I must not be late. My boss made quite a point of my being there at exactly eight-thirty."

At eight-twenty-seven Suzanne turned the knob of number 206 and peeked in. Penny wasn't at her desk. Holding the door so it wouldn't slam, she quietly entered the room, and feeling somewhat like a thief, she crossed over to the office area, and glanced down the empty hall. She stood at the low gate and wondered if she should go in, or wait until Penny came. The phone's shrill jangle made her gasp. She waited until the second ring, then stepped decisively through the gate and answered it.

"Mr. Wheatley's office." Her voice was clear, her tone businesslike.

"Hi. Is that you, Suzanne? This is Penny. Boy, am I glad you're there. Listen, my car's sick."

"Oh, I'm sorry."

"I'll be there just as soon as the auto club gets it going, okay? Tell Mr. Wheatley for me, please?"

"Of course. Is there anything I should be doing?"

"Well . . . Oh! There's the tow truck. Gotta run. See you."

Suzanne looked at the silent phone, then replaced it. She sighed, and looked around. What should she do? She was certain Mr. Wheatley was in his office, or else the front door would have been locked. Should she let him know she was here? She moved over to her shining, new desk and smiled. *It's really mine. I'm a legal secretary in a brand new office, for a very handsome up-and-coming attorney.*

She pulled the new IBM typewriter up into place and examined it. She opened a drawer, found paper and put a sheet in the typewriter. She turned on the power and typed the practice line, *Now is the time for all good men to come to the aid of their party.*

"And now is the time for all good secretaries to come to the aid of their bosses," Justin Wheatley boomed in a courtroom voice directly behind her.

She jumped and yelped at the same time, looking up at him over her shoulder. "I didn't hear you come in." Her heart was beating like a frightened bird's.

"Didn't mean to startle you." He smiled at her. "Where's Penny?" He began to look through some papers in Penny's "In" box.

19

Suzanne gave him Penny's message, but he didn't seem to listen. Suddenly he looked up from reading and stared at her. Their eyes locked. She squirmed inwardly, but managed to look poised and confident.

"Congratulations," he said. "You weren't late."

"I'm usually on time."

"For your sake, I hope you're always on time."

Suzanne felt the blood rise in her cheeks. Naturally, she would try not to be late, but hadn't he ever heard of the human element? With two children anything could happen . . . and with Crystal it usually did.

"I have a lot of dictation to give you," he said, "but stay out here until Penny shows. When she comes, bring your steno pad to my office." He walked toward the hall, then looked back at her. His mouth was lifted on one side and his emerald eyes looked amused. "While you're waiting for Penny, feel free to practice your typewriter exercises."

Indignation flared again for a moment, then she nodded at him. "Well, thank you, Mr. Boss." He walked away and she couldn't tell how he took her quip. Had she been too impudent?

She was still worrying about it when Penny rushed in, breathless and beautiful. Her mahogany curls were caught up off her neck with a ribbon, and long tendrils bounced around her face and neck, accenting her pearl-like complexion. Her bright green dress fell in smooth folds.

"Man! Am I glad to get here. Did you explain to Mr. Wheatley? He'll probably fire me."

Suzanne smiled. "He didn't seem to be angry."

"Really? Thank goodness. He's got this thing." Penny lowered her voice to a whisper. "I think he must have lost a case once because of somebody being late. Well, anyhow, this is the first time, and I couldn't help it." She pushed her gigantic canvas bag in a drawer.

"What was wrong with your car?"

"I have to get a new starter. I don't know how much it'll cost."

Suzanne shook her head sympathetically. Recently, she had had a hard time getting the station wagon started and knew it needed work, but she had no idea where to take it or how to pay for it. Del had always taken care of the cars. She picked up a new steno notebook and motioned toward the hall. "He told me to come in as soon as you got here."

"Right." Penny's smile was dazzling as she gave Suzanne a thumbs up sign.

Suzanne tapped on Justin Wheatley's door and rested her hand on the knob. It had been months since she had given herself a manicure, and the bright polish jumped out at her.

"Come in," he said, after a half a minute. As before, he kept reading. She crossed the room quietly and sat in the same chair she had occupied. Was it only yesterday?

"Okay, Susie," he said at last, still not looking at her. He shuffled papers, then unfolded a blue-backed document. "The first thing I want to get out of the way is Vincent Marino's new will."

Marino. Where had she heard that name?

"He was in yesterday," the lawyer went on. "And I expect to get a pretty nice fee from him in regard to a pending suit, so—" he looked at her and assumed a theatrical expression of martyrdom "—we must do our best on the mundane."

Of course. Mr. Marino was the other man she had seen here yesterday. As she sat quietly, notebook and pen poised, she recalled Mr. Marino's dark good looks and wondered why he would be involved in a lawsuit.

"By the way, Susie, how do you like you job so far?"

Wide-eyed, she looked at her boss. "Well, Mr. Wheatley, so far—"

21

"Call me Justin. Since you're two years older than I am you don't need to call me 'mister,' all right?" His eyes sparkled and his mouth threatened to smile.

She blushed. *This man certainly has a way of making me feel at a disadvantage.* She looked down at her notebook to escape his penetrating stare. *He's probably counting the wrinkles in my crow's feet.*

"Okay," he said, suddenly businesslike. "Penny can show you the files and our standard will, so I don't need to dictate all the first part, about revoking all other wills, et cetera, okay?"

She hoped it was okay. She hadn't done any wills while working for the district attorney in Colorado.

"Marino's wife died three years ago," Justin began. "Strange, too. She was only thirty-seven. Had some kind of heart disease. Anyway, he wants to update his will. Oh, and make a note. I want you to call my former partner. Penny can give you the number. Tell one of the secretaries over there that Marino is drawing up a new will with me. Just a courtesy so they don't have a lot of dead wood in their files."

He studied the document before him, which Suzanne assumed was a copy of Mr. Marino's old will. A good secretary didn't stare at her boss while he was gathering his thoughts, she knew, but she couldn't resist some quick peeks. He was a strange, yet almost beautiful man. He reminded her of Michelangelo's statue of David, except that he was so alive. The scent of his pleasant-smelling shaving lotion also reminded her of something, but she couldn't call it to mind.

He cleared his throat, and she looked down quickly at her notebook, and got a grip on her pen.

"Under Article Eleven make this entry: 'I give, devise, and bequeath all of my Estate as described in Article Three as follows: Item One. If my daughter, Carlotta Madge Marino, survives the distribution of my estate, I give my entire said estate to her."

Suzanne scribbled furiously. Some of her outlines

22

were clumsy and awkward, but she was able to keep pace with him.

"Item Two. If my daughter and I should die simultaneously, then in such event I give my entire estate to my granddaughter, Kristen Kay Marshall.

"Twelve: I nominate my daughter as Executor of this Will to serve without bond. If she is not living, then I nominate and appoint Justin David Wheatley as Executor. And so forth and so forth." He looked at her. "Okay?"

Suzanne nodded just as the buzzer sounded. Justin answered, listened a moment, then covered the mouthpiece. He looked at Suzanne. "Why don't you get started on the will? We can take care of this other stuff later."

Seated at her desk, Suzanne tried to appear calm and competent, but her stomach quivered, and in spite of the advertising claims for her deodorant, she felt damp under her arms. Penny showed her the files and gave her a sample will.

"I wonder how many copies I should type?" Suzanne said as she took out legal size paper.

"We always use the Xerox. I don't think there's any carbon paper here. At least I've never seen any."

"Oh, the Xerox, of course." Suzanne put the paper in the typewriter. When she placed her fingers on the keyboard she could feel them trembling, and she hoped Penny would turn around and do something besides look at her. She stared at her shorthand notes. The outlines might as well have been Egyptian hieroglyphics. She closed her eyes and prayed one word: *Help!*

"Suzanne?" Penny's voice seemed to jab her like the tip of a knife. "Since you've here to cover the phone," she said, "I'm going down to the snack bar and get some hot chocolate. You want anything?"

Suzanne hadn't eaten breakfast and probably

should get something, but her appetite was gone. "No thanks, Penny." She looked up and smiled. "And take your time." *Please*, she added under her breath.

When Penny returned from her break Suzanne had figured out her notes and felt reasonably sure she was doing all right on Mr. Marino's will.

By noon she had completed it and was ready for Mr. Wheatley—Justin, she corrected herself—to see it. Before she could buzz his office, the front door opened. Mr. Marino barged in and crossed quickly to Penny's desk.

"Hi, Mr. Marino." Penny grinned warmly. "Boy, you look like you're in a hurry."

"I am. Is Justin in?" He glanced at Suzanne and nodded.

"Sure," Penny answered, reaching for the phone. "I'll get him for you."

"Never mind," Mr. Marino called as he strode down the hall. "I know where he is."

"Wow." Penny looked dumbfounded. "I'm not supposed to let people do that."

"I know. He's a huge man, isn't he?"

"He sure is."

Suzanne looked at her watch. "When do we go to lunch?"

"Let's go now." Penny jumped up. "I'm starved. There's a McDonald's real close, and there's a fish place that has good sandwiches, and—"

"Oh, I'm sorry, Penny, but I'd planned to go home during the lunch hour so I can see my kids."

"Oh, that's right. I'd forgotten for a moment that you had children." Penny took her bag out of the drawer and walked into the reception room. Suzanne picked up her purse and followed her. She thought about inviting Penny home for lunch, but Harriet wouldn't be prepared. "Someday soon I'll invite you over at noon so you can meet my children."

"Neat! I'd like to see them."

"I just happen to have their pictures," Suzanne said with a laugh when Mr. Marino and Justin came into the reception room.

"What's to keep us from taking these two beautiful women to lunch, Justin?" Mr. Marino's voice was deep and cordial, and he seemed more relaxed than he had been a few moments before.

Suzanne looked over at Penny, who began to beam with pleasure.

"Sounds like a terrific idea," Justin answered, "especially if it's on your expense account." Then he added, "Just kidding. I'd be delighted to take us all to lunch. How about the Velvet Turtle?"

"Oooh," Penny murmured and raised an eyebrow at Suzanne.

"I almost forgot," Justin said. "Mr. Marino, I'd like to introduce my new secretary, Susie—Suzanne Forrest."

"Suzanne." Vincent Marino made her name sound like a caress as he took her hand and held it firmly in his. She had to tip her head back to look at him, and for a second it seemed as though the floor moved under her feet as she gazed into his dark, liquid eyes.

She pulled her hand back abruptly and looked at Justin. "I'm sorry I can't go to lunch with you today."

"Why not?"

"I . . . it's just that . . . well, I told my sitter I'd be home at noon and see the children."

"You can call her, can't you?" Justin held her with his eyes.

This lunch must be important to him, she thought. The children were certainly being well cared for. She shrugged. "Of course."

As she waited for Harriet to answer the phone, she glanced at Mr. Marino. He certainly didn't look like a grandfather. In his tan pants and pullover sweater he looked as young as a college student. And what had happened to her when she looked in his eyes a moment ago? It had been like an earth tremor, and for a second she had almost forgotten where she was. Harriet's "Hello" made her turn away from him so she could concentrate. When she hung up she turned and smiled at him. Then she looked at Justin. "It's all right."

"Good," he said, "Lets go."

Penny and Suzanne preceded the men out the door and to the elevator. Penny, who never seemed to be out of conversation, kept turning around to look at Justin as she told him about having to get a new starter for her car.

"Well, if some of you women would ever learn that a car has to have something besides gas once in a while, you wouldn't have these problems," Justin said.

"That's true," Mr. Marino joined in. "I have to keep on my daughter all the time to even get her to have the car serviced."

I guess his daughter is old enough to drive, Suzanne thought. She leaned against the side of the elevator and covertly looked at him. Standing so close to him she could see, even this early in the day, a beginning of five o'clock shadow. He smelled good, more like soap and the outdoors than aftershave. His hands were twice as big as hers, and looked as though he had done hard labor. *I can't believe this,* she thought, *but I actually feel petite beside him.*

"Well, anyway," Penny continued, "the mechanic said he'd be done by five tonight."

"That's good." Suzanne felt sorry for her. Justin's tone of voice had been harsh. "Do you want me to drive you to the garage?"

"Oh, no. It's in that place cater-cornered from here."

"Speaking of cars," Vincent Marino said as he opened the wide, plate-glass door, "can we go to lunch in your car, Justin? I drove the Porsche over, and there's no room in it."

Justin laughed and clapped his hands together. "I was just getting ready to ask you the same thing. There's no room in my Corvette."

Suzanne stared from one to the other. Penny's mouth was open. "Does this mean we don't get to go to the Velvet Turtle?" She sounded like a little girl.

Suzanne thought of her station wagon. How much junk was in the back? No matter, she had to offer. "If you don't mind a slightly beaten-up Toyota, I'll be glad to drive us."

When she unlocked the car she shuddered. Randy's comic books were all over the back seat, there was an old diaper bag on the floor and a couple of cartons of empty Pepsi bottles, but the men didn't comment as they got in, and matter-of-factly shoved the comic books to the center. She hoped the seat wasn't dusty enough to show on their pants. Penny rode in front with her, chattering about a new choir director at their church. Suzanne started to ask her about the church, but she decided to concentrate on her driving. It was only a short distance on the freeway, but it seemed forever. She was miserable, with a brand new boss and one of his clients in the back seat, watching every move she made. At the restaurant, however, Vincent Marino helped her out of the car, and remarked softly, "You're an excellent driver."

"Thank you, Mr. Marino."

"Suzanne," his lips tarried over her name, "won't you please call me Vincent? I'm going to be coming to the office a lot, and 'mister' makes me seem ancient. I feel too old anyway."

Suzanne laughed and her eyes flashed up at him. "I know how you feel," she said. She looked over at Justin. "I'm older than my boss."

"You couldn't be!" Vincent seemed genuinely amazed.

"Yes, she is," Justin said. "But that's all right. Older women have a place in life."

Vincent looked down at Suzanne and shook his head. "Well, regardless of her age, from now on, I want all of you to drop the mister."

He walked beside Suzanne toward the entrance, and Penny, suddenly quiet, seemed awed as she walked along beside Justin.

Suzanne had never been to the Velvet Turtle, and was astonished at the abundance and variety of greenery. "It's like walking into an arboretum," she exclaimed.

"Look at the size of those Boston ferns," Penny chimed in. "Wonder how they do it? My fern is smaller now than the day I bought it."

Suzanne's lips were slightly parted, and her eyes dreamy, as she took in the scene. The white table cloths hung almost to the floor, and lighted candles made a soft glow everywhere. The hostess led them to a table toward the back of the dining room, and Suzanne took a chair against the wall. She thought Penny would sit by her, but Vincent eased his big body down next to hers As she studied the menu she could feel her heart pounding. *Murphy's Law*, she thought. *An opportunity to eat filet mignon, and I'm too nervous to swallow.*

CHAPTER 3

AN ATTRACTIVE WAITRESS in an enticing blue uniform brought crystal glasses of iced water, then asked, "May I bring you something from the bar?"

"Yes," Vincent said, smiling at Suzanne. "What'll it be?"

She shook her head quickly. Because of Del's increasing overindulgence during the past two years, she had come to detest any form of alcohol. "Nothing for me, thank you."

"A glass of rosé?"

"Coffee would be fine."

"Penny?"

"Nothing for me, either, thank you."

"You've got a couple of saints, Justin." He looked up at the waitress. "I'll have a margarita. How about you, Counselor?"

Justin pursed his lips and frowned. "I seldom drink. But," he grinned boyishly, "I wouldn't want you to drink alone." He turned to the waitress. "Bring me a margarita, too."

After methodically studying the menu, Penny said, "I'm just going to have a dinner salad."

29

"A dinner salad?" Justin repeated. "Is that all?"

"And a chocolate mousse," she added.

Everyone laughed except Penny. "What's so funny?" Her sapphire eyes were wide. "I love chocolate mousse. If I just have a salad, then I can have the dessert without getting too many calories."

"But that's not good for you," Justin said. "You'd better learn to take care of your body." His eyes slowly explored her form. "It has to last you all your life."

"That's right," Vincent agreed, smiling. He leaned toward Suzanne and spoke softly, "You're not having a dinner salad, I hope."

Although he didn't touch her, Suzanne was aware of his bigness, his magnetic warmth. The thought occurred to her that it would be very nice to have someone like him to lean on, to rest in his strength.

"I'm really not hungry." She read the menu carefully, not trusting herself to look at him. "I think I'll have a bowl of soup."

"Soup!" He looked appalled. "Justin, can't you do something with your secretary? She needs more than soup."

Justin shrugged, and Suzanne shook her head firmly. It had been a nerve-wracking morning. Bad enough that it was her first day on the job, working for a handsome yet unpredictable boss, but then to meet the captivating Vincent Marino and then having to chauffeur the two dynamic strangers. The strain had left her too self-conscious and quivery to concentrate on food.

"No, really." She looked at him then, and was caught in his gaze. His dark, liquid eyes were a whirlpool, making her feel giddy, off-balance, as though she were on board a ship. As she fought for control, she hoped the others didn't notice. She forced herself to look at people across the room, the exotic plants, anything except those hypnotic eyes. At the same time, she put her left hand down at her side. The sight of her rings always reminded her she had failed—and right now, she didn't want to think about that.

She decided instead to center her thoughts on the lunch. Turning to Penny, she started to ask her a question when she realized Penny had her eyes closed. In an instant, however, Penny opened them and smiled brightly at Suzanne, then began to attack her salad ravenously.

She was praying, Suzanne thought. The realization touched her, and for a second or two she had a strange longing in her heart. In her teens she had given her heart to Christ; but Del wasn't interested in spiritual matters, and over the years she had felt the new life in her slowly being squelched. Without warning, hot tears threatened to spill over, and she blinked hard as she looked down at her soup.

"Here's to you," Vincent said, and held his stemmed glass toward her. She shivered as she watched him drink the cocktail. He touched his lips with a large cloth napkin and said, "Now, young lady, I want you to taste this steak. Women need a lot of red meat in their diet." He placed a generous piece of steak on her bread plate, and for a second Suzanne thought he was going to cut it up. "I'm always on Carla, that's my daughter, to eat food, instead of," he motioned with his fork at Penny's salad, "all that rabbit fodder."

Suzanne laughed, but took a bite of the meat. She felt foolish and juvenile under his intense gaze. She scarcely knew this man, yet here she was, obeying him like a good little girl. Still, Vincent Marino was not a person to argue with. Besides, he *was* an important client.

"How did you like it?"

"Delicious," she answered honestly.

"Want more?"

She laughed. "No."

"Just like Carla. Afraid you'll gain an ounce."

"How old is your daughter?" Suzanne asked.

He smiled down at her, his eyes half-closed. "You had to ask, didn't you?" He pushed some mushrooms around on his plate. "I hate to admit it in the company of beautiful women, but she's nineteen."

Suzanne looked at his face. Of course the light was dim, but he looked so young. She calculated in her head. If he had been about twenty when his daughter was born, he would be . . .

"I was forty in December . . . if that's what you're trying to figure out," he chuckled.

She opened her mouth, then closed it.

"I hate to interrupt," Justin said, "but to make this lunch a legal deduction, I'll have to discuss some business." He leaned back, and with arms outstretched he placed his palms on the table. "So, Vincent, with the news you brought me today I think we've got them."

The youthful smile on Vincent's face disappeared. Suzanne saw the muscle in his jaw bulge as he clenched his teeth. His tone of voice became harsh. "I hope so. Those people have pushed me around long enough."

"Anyone care for dessert?" Their waitress was holding a tray full of assorted cakes and pies.

"Yes," Penny said. "Where's my chocolate mousse?"

The waitress looked stricken. "Oh! I forgot. I'll get it right away. Pie, cake, anyone?"

Justin waved her away, and turned back to Vincent. "The only thing that might shoot us down would be if they brought in a genuine environmentalist who could find something," he went on. "Of course, in that case, the other firm couldn't build either."

Vincent threw his napkin on the table. "What could they find to protect in a ten-acre strawberry patch?"

"You'd be surprised what some of those people call wilderness acres."

With a flourish, the waitress placed a huge portion of chocolate mousse in front of Penny. Her eyes widened with pleasure and awe.

"I'm not sure I can eat all this."

"Let's hope not." Justin looked at the concoction with disgust.

Suzanne smiled and looked up at Vincent. "Is it out of line for me to ask what's wrong? I mean, why you're going to sue?"

Vincent looked at Justin, who nodded. "She'll be doing all the typing, anyway."

Vincent lifted his hands in a short, helpless gesture. "I'm a building contractor. I own ten acres in Walnut Heights, on which I have intended for several years to build condominiums when I had the financing." He paused and turned slightly, so he could look directly at her. "A year ago I was ready to go, had my plans approved, all my subcontractors lined up. Then they stopped me."

"Who's they?" she asked.

"A group of homeowners in that area. They claimed that construction would violate certain environmental concerns."

Suzanne frowned slightly. She had heard plenty about the environment from Selena, but she hadn't really listened. Of course, she believed that wildlife should be protected, but she had never given much thought as to how this should be accomplished.

"Where is your land?" she asked.

He gestured vaguely. "Not too far from here. There are homes and businesses all around. And my property isn't big enough to become a preserve, or even much of a park. Besides that, it's mine!" He drank his coffee and leaned back. "The homeowners to the east of my land are the ones who have brought the action against me, and if there were no other homes or buildings bordering it, I could see their complaint, but to the north is the freeway, and to the south are single dwelling homes, and directly west the land's been zoned for R-2 and Industrial.''

"I still believe we could go with that alone," Justin interjected, "but your new information will clinch it."

"What new information?" Penny asked, without looking up from her dessert.

Vincent glanced at her, but looked at Suzanne when he answered. "I've known for a long time that one of the homeowner's has a brother who is a building contractor in San Bernardino, but in the Building Department this morning—and only because the clerk had me confused with this other joker—I found out he's requested a permit to build condos on the property adjacent to mine." He paused and his eyes were smoldering.

Penny scooped up the last of the chocolate mousse. "I don't get it."

Suzanne's green eyes gleamed. "The contractor talked his brother into starting this environment thing against you, so he could build there."

"Right," Vincent said.

"But it's probably more complex than that," Justin added. He looked at Vincent, whose black brows were drawn together like a thunder cloud. Suzanne shivered. *I'd hate to have him against me*, she thought. Justin continued in a confident tone, "We're going to look for evidence that will prove the home-owners have formed an association, or a company with the gentleman from San Bernardino." He winked and nodded. "We'll find it, too." He looked at Penny's empty dessert dish and closed his eyes briefly. "Penny, I can't believe you ate all that."

She grinned up at him. "I told you, Mr. Wheatley. I love chocolate mousse."

Vincent stared at the empty dish, then laughed. "People say all men are just boys at heart, but I say

34

all women are just little girls." He chuckled and patted Suzanne's cheek, then looked at his watch. "I've got to run."

"We've got to get back, too." Justin stood up and helped Penny to her feet. "By the way, I want the three of us to have different lunch hours. I want that phone covered at all times."

On the way out to the parking lot Vincent again walked beside Suzanne, instead of Justin, which made her feel slightly uncomfortable, yet pleased. For one frantic moment, after they got to the car, she thought she had lost the keys, but found them in the section of her purse where she always kept them. *This man has some strange effect on me*, she thought, as she unlocked the station wagon.

Suzanne left the Toyota in the driveway instead of putting it in the garage. She would have to take Harriet home, and probably go to the store for milk and bread. She berated herself for not being more organized. Just last night she had gone out because Crystal needed baby food, and then noticed this morning that the milk supply was low. *I used to be organized*, she thought. *But that was B.C.—Before Crystal*. She smiled wryly. That little character had certainly turned her world upside down. Some of her friends said their second baby was much easier to care for, but Suzanne's experience had been the opposite. Randy had been a much better baby. He had never given her any trouble.

As she got out of the car Randy banged out the front door and raced toward her. She bent down to hug and kiss him. There was dried milk on his upper lip and his head felt hot and damp.

"I've been watching for you, Mom."

"Have you, darling?" She took his hand and they walked toward the front door. "You feel hot. Have you been running?"

35

"Yep. I ran all the way from Jimmy's house."

"Jimmy's house? I thought you were waiting for me." Suzanne looked down at him with love and teasing in her eyes.

"I was. But I was at Jimmy's house first. Grandma said I could stay until five-fifteen, and then you'd come home."

"I didn't miss it by much, did I?" She tousled his hair. "You're going to have to have a haircut Saturday." She sighed at the thought of all the things that would have to be done on the weekend. Del was supposed to visit the children. Maybe he would take Randy for a haircut.

Crystal began to whine and reach for her the moment they walked in the door.

"There's your mommy," Harriet said, struggling to get out of Del's big chair with the heavy baby in her arms.

"Here, let me take her." Suzanne dropped her bag on the floor and crossed quickly to the baby. She shut her eyes as she held the baby close. "Oh, you smell so good! Mmmm!" She rained kisses on the baby's head, cheeks, and neck. "I missed you so much." She stood rocking her back and forth. "Was she good, Harriet?"

"Just fine. They both were."

Randy leaned against Suzanne's leg. "Do you have to go to work tomorrow?" He looked up at her with sad eyes.

"Yes sir." She put her arm around his bony shoulders. "I surely do. Have to make some money to take care of my darlings."

"I could ask daddy to give you some money."

Suzanne and Harriet exchanged glances. Del hadn't been very good about giving Suzanne money, and Harriet had ended up buying groceries a few times since Suzanne had been so short of cash.

"Who's hungry in this house?" Harriet asked quickly.

"Me!" Randy yelled, apparently forgetting about money and his dad.

"Well, I'm glad, because I just happen to have a skillet full of fried chicken."

"Is that what smells so heavenly?" Suzanne gently disengaged herself from Randy, and started toward the kitchen, with Crystal hanging on to her neck like a baby monkey.

After dinner Suzanne leaned back, took a deep breath, and smiled at Harriet. "I wonder if I'll ever learn to fry chicken the way you do."

"There's nothing to it." Harriet looked down and smiled. Then she looked up at Suzanne. "That reminds me, how was your lunch today?"

"Oh, fine." Her tone was noncommittal. She didn't want to talk about lunch for fear she would reveal her feelings. She had thought about Vincent a great deal during the afternoon hours. When he got out of her station wagon he shook hands with Justin, smiled at Penny, and then gave Suzanne a look that caused her stomach to lurch. Or had she only imagined he looked deeply into her eyes? But it hadn't been imagination when he squeezed her arm. "I'll see all of you in a day or so," he had said, then sprinted away toward his car. It had been difficult to concentrate on Justin's dictation in the afternoon, and even harder to transcribe it. Vincent Marino's deeply tanned face and luminous eyes kept popping up in her mind.

"What are you staring at, Mommy?"

Randy's voice brought her out of her reverie.

"Nothing. I guess I'm tired."

"You go put your feet up and watch TV," Harriet said. "I'll do these few dishes."

"Oh, no," Suzanne jumped to her feet. "You've done so much already. In fact, I'd better get you home. It's dark."

Harriet faced her with a worried expression. "Why

don't I just spend the night?" She paused, waiting for Suzanne's answer. "You can lend me a nightie, and then tomorrow, after Randy goes to kindergarten, I can put Crystal in the stroller and walk to my place for a change of clothes." She looked at Suzanne expectantly. "We walked to the little store on the corner today for bread and milk."

A warning sounded in Suzanne's mind, but she could think of no reason to refuse her mother-in-law. In fact, it seemed a sensible solution. She was tired, and it would take all the strength she could muster to get Crystal ready for bed, read Randy a story, and get her clothes ready for the next day.

"And to tell the truth," Harriet said, "it'll be easier on me in the morning."

"Of course." Suzanne smiled faintly. "Thank you for being willing to stay."

As the two women did the dishes together Suzanne was grateful that Harriet did most of the talking. She filled her in on all of Crystal's doings, which included wriggling out of the strap on the highchair, then standing up on the tray while Harriet was heating some soup.

"I tell you, when I turned around and saw her, I was afraid I was going to have a heart attack." Harriet didn't look afraid, but wore the indulgent expression of a grandparent. "That child is always two steps ahead of me."

Suzanne nodded. Then she frowned. "I hope this isn't going to be too hard on you, Harriet."

"Oh, no." She answered so quickly it startled Suzanne. "I'm happy to be able to help out."

"Were there any calls about the ad?"

Harriet ducked her head and vigorously scrubbed a pan. "Don't worry about it. I'm not suffering." She turned her back and wiped the stove carefully. "Anyway, you'd have to pay a sitter quite a bit."

"Well, I certainly intend to pay you."

"Now I won't have that. Del's father left me well fixed. I don't need money."

Suzanne was too tired to argue, but she felt like a fly trapped in a spider's web. Evidently, Harriet wanted to move in, and she couldn't think of any reason to keep her from it. They finished the dishes in silence. Suzanne folded the tea towel and hung it over the towel rack. As she moved toward the dining room, she spoke listlessly.

"I guess you could sleep on Randy's bed. I'll change the sheets."

"No, I'm not going to take his room away from him, either. Just get me a blanket for the couch."

"You can't sleep on the couch!"

"Sue, now don't argue with me. I'll sleep fine. Randy needs his own room." She took off her apron and smiled. "There's no sense in having your entire routine upset, just for the few days I'll be here."

"Well, okay, if you're sure you can sleep. You could have my bed."

"Honey, please quit worrying. You need your sleep more than I do."

Even though she was tired, Suzanne enjoyed getting Crystal ready for bed. "What an adorable, precious baby you are," she told her. "You're even more beautiful tonight than you were last night, you little doll."

Crystal grinned, showing all her teeth.

"Mommy's going to rock you, and give you your bottle, and read to Randy at the same time. Won't that be fun?" As she lifted the baby she called out, "Randy? Are you in your p.j.'s? Hurry up, and bring a book. And get Crystal's bottle." She went to the living room and sank down in the rocker.

Randy wanted her to read the Star Wars book.

"Not again, Randy! That's what I read every night."

He nodded solemnly. "I like it best."

"I don't think all that outer space stuff is good for kids," Harriet commented, already seated on the couch, knitting. "Do you?"

Suzanne shrugged, pushed Crystal back on her arm, gave her the bottle, and, rocking gently, she began to read. As she mechanically read the words, she began to think of Vincent Marino. It was unbelievable how young he was—for the father of a nineteen-year-old daughter and a grandfather! She thought of the terms of his will. There was no mention of any other children. Was the daughter divorced? Nineteen was young, but she could have a child and be divorced.

"Mommy." Randy's voice made Crystal jump. "You left out part of it."

"Shh. I think she's asleep," Suzanne murmured. "You go to the bathroom now, and don't forget to get a drink. Then hop in bed." She struggled to stand up without waking the baby. "I'll be in to pray with you."

When she leaned over the crib, Crystal rolled out of her arms like a heavy sack of grain. She put a light blanket over her, and tiptoed from the room.

As she sat on Randy's bed and listened to his prayer, she remembered Penny at lunchtime. *She must be very religious*, she thought. You don't often see people pray in restaurants. She kissed Randy goodnight, then went to the bathroom to shower.

Since Del moved out she had gotten into the habit of putting the children to bed, showering, then watching TV until she got sleepy. Sometimes she stayed up past midnight, but she couldn't do that tonight since Harriet would be on the couch. Maybe it was just as well. Now that she was working, she needed sleep, too.

After her shower she wrapped herself in a towel, dashed to the bedroom and put on a faded nightshirt. She opened a bureau drawer and took out her best nightie for Harriet, a faded blue waltz-length gown, with lots of lace at the top. She had received it at one of her showers, and Del had loved it. But the last time she had put it on, he had stared at her, then gone into the living room to watch TV.

She draped the gown over a chair, then began to look through the closet, trying to decide what to wear to work. She had lost several pounds since Del left, but she still had a few more to lose before she could get into some of her pre-Crystal clothes. She selected a lavender flowered print that always looked nice, twisted the metal neck of the hanger and hung it over the closet door. She picked up the gown and started for the living room. On the way she opened the linen closet and took out sheets, a pillow and case, and a blanket.

"I'll make your bed for you, Harriet," she said.

"No, no. I'll make it myself. Are you going to watch TV?"

"No." Her answer was too short. "I'm tired, I'm going right to bed."

"Oh." Harriet seemed disappointed. "This seems like it'll be a good movie. Well, if I'm not up in the morning, be sure and wake me."

"Okay. Goodnight."

In her room she wondered why she had been so curt and contrary. She always watched TV. *But I don't want to watch TV with her. Not tonight.*

As she stood at the dresser brushing her hair, her diamond ring caught the light. She slowly put down the brush and touched her white gold wedding rings. She hadn't been with Del when he chose them. Like so many other things, he had bought the rings because he liked them and had gotten a good buy. She looked at them closely. The diamond was half a carat, and had two smaller stones on each side. The wedding band had five, five-point diamonds in it. It was an impressive set, but Suzanne had never liked it. If she had been allowed to choose, she would have selected a solitaire and a yellow gold band.

41

She twisted and pulled at the rings. She almost never took them off because they fit so tightly. By pouring on hand lotion, she finally worked them off. Holding them by thumb and forefinger, she dangled them over the jewelry box. She bit her lip and frowned. Then taking a deep breath, she dropped the rings, and quickly shut the lid.

CHAPTER 4

IT HAD BEEN THREE WEEKS since Suzanne quit wearing her rings, yet there was still a pale circle on her finger. The first day without them she wore a silver turquoise ring, a souvenir from Arizona, but when she saw Penny glance at it, she felt flustered, and put it in her purse. She hoped Penny hadn't really noticed it.

Maybe I'm not ready to admit being single, she thought. Certainly not because she still felt anything for Del, but she didn't want to talk about her failure. Besides, she didn't want anyone else trying to fix her up with dates. It was bad enough to have Selena ask her every few days if she had met "anybody" yet. She didn't want anybody, and she would probably never marry again.

Still, Vincent Marino was often in her thoughts. He came into the office every few days, either to sign papers or confer with Justin, but other than flashing his heart-melting smile her way, he didn't pay her any particular attention. When he was in Justin's office, Suzanne would surreptitiously take out her compact and check her makeup and hair. Then, if she could think of a legitimate excuse to interrupt the men, she would take up her notebook or papers in a stiff, businesslike manner, not daring to look at Penny, walk briskly into Justin's office and tap lightly on the door. Her heart would pound as she waited for his "Come in."

"I'm a fool," she always told herself. "A school-girl fool."

Inside Justin's office, she would barely look at Vincent, pretending to be interested only in the business she had brought in for Justin. But she was so aware of his masculinity and good looks, she had even thought of touching him! She allowed herself to imagine brushing his shoulder as she leaned across the desk, or the fantasy of having him leave Justin's office just as she did, and they would walk up the short hallway together. He would take her hand and say, "Let's have lunch together. I've missed you." But in three weeks it hadn't happened.

This morning, on the way to work, Suzanne felt cross. For one thing, actually the main thing, she was tired of having Harriet there all the time. Yet, how could she complain? Harriet kept the house neat, and there was always a delicious meal at night. She kept Randy warm and dry on cold rainy days, and Crystal was always clean and happy when she came home. She probably didn't even realize what a help Harriet was.

But in spite of those pluses, she would give anything for some time alone. *I'm always with people,* she thought, as she wiped steam off the windshield with a tissue. *I never have a minute to just sit in my own living room and relax.* Although Harriet seemed to be trying to do everything in her power to make Suzanne comfortable, between her and the children and the job she felt smothered. "The only time I'm really by myself is when I'm in the bathroom, in bed, or in this car," she said aloud.

She didn't realize how cross she looked when she sat down at her desk. Penny's blue eyes were compassionate as she asked, "What's wrong?"

Suzanne looked over at her, startled. "Does it show that much?"

"Well, it's just that you look so . . ."

"Grumpy?" Suzanne suggested.

Penny shrugged. "Usually you're smiling."

"I'll admit I don't feel like smiling this morning." Suzanne's green eyes flashed and she slammed her purse into the drawer. "I've got mother-in-law problems."

"Oh." Penny nodded wisely.

"It's not what you think," Suzanne said, quickly. "She's a lovely person, and she likes me. And she loves the kids. That I know for sure." Penny listened, her head tipped slightly and hands resting quietly in her lap. "I've never told you," Suzanne continued, "but I'm getting a divorce."

Penny looked down. "I sort of figured that," she said and gestured toward Suzanne's left hand.

"You know I have the two children—"

"Yeah, and I certainly hope I get to see them soon."

"I ran an ad in the *Highlander* for three weeks for a baby sitter, but there wasn't one response. So my mother-in-law is living with me now, to take care of the kids. It's really thoughtful of her," Suzanne closed her eyes for a moment and sighed, "but I hate it. Yet I don't know what to do."

Penny shook her head. "I really feel for you. After I went to Biola for two years, I tried to live with my folks again but I couldn't."

"You live alone?"

"Sure do. I have a little apartment right on Hacienda Boulevard. I love it."

"Well, anyway, you know what it's like to come home beat, and not want to talk, and I don't mind talking to Randy, that's my son. I mean, he goes on and on about his friends, and all I have to do is listen and say 'uh, huh.' And he goes to bed early. But I don't feel like talking or listening to her for three or four hours every evening.'' Suddenly tears glistened in her eyes and she compressed her lips. "Oh, for Pete's sake!" She turned slightly and wiped her eyes. "I feel ashamed for talking to you. She's really a sweet lady.''

"Maybe you just need to do something different for a change, Suzanne.'' Penny leaned forward compassionately. "Why don't you come home with me tonight?'' Her eyes sparkled. "We could eat at McDonald's or take chicken home, and after we eat, you could sit in on a neat sharing group that meets at my apartment on Tuesday nights.''

Suzanne blotted her eyes and nose with a tissue. She looked at Penny. "A sharing group?'' One eyebrow lifted.

"Yeah. It's really great.'' Penny flipped her curly auburn hair back over her shoulders. "John Dempsey, a man from our church, shares some thoughts from the Bible, then the rest of us tell some of the ways God has helped us during the week.'' Her eyes were clear and level as she looked at Suzanne. "I'm sure you'd like it.''

Suzanne continued to stare at her a moment, then sighed and turned to her typewriter. "I can't come tonight,'' she said, sounding more brusque than she had intended. She turned to look at Penny. "I promised Harriet, that's my mother-in-law, I'd buy groceries tonight.''

Penny smiled graciously. "That's okay. But maybe next week.''

"What kind of church do you go to?''

"You mean what brand?'' Penny laughed gently. "I actually don't know if it's any denomination. It's called 'Better Life Fellowship,' and the pastor is

46

young, and really knows the Bible. His wife is darling, and they have two little kids." As Penny spoke, there was a light in her eyes and a glow on her face.

"How did you start going there?" Suzanne asked.

Penny leaned back in her chair and crossed her legs. "Hmmm! I'll have to think a minute." She compressed her lips and looked up at the ceiling. "I started going there about a year ago, right after I broke up with my boyfriend." She bit her lip and looked down for a moment, then smiled impishly. "Don't worry. I'm all over him. It just wasn't meant to be. Anyway, Tim, that was his name, Tim and I were attending Christ Community, you know, it's that big church on the hill over on Milna?" Suzanne nodded. "Well, Tim and I were engaged to be married, and the church had just hired him part-time for the youth work, when we broke up, so naturally he had to stay at Community. 'This church ain't big enough for th' both of us,' I thought, so I started going to Better Life because it was closer."

"That must have taken incredible courage. I don't think I could start going to a church alone."

"It was only hard the first couple of Sundays. They seemed to love me right from the start. Now I know everybody, and there's always something going on for the singles. I sing in the choir, too."

"Sounds like a nice church."

"Oh, it is. I just love it. I don't know what I'd do without my church friends. Do you go to church?"

Suzanne had been gazing at Penny, admiring her courage and thinking how pretty she was. Now she suddenly felt uncomfortable. "No. I used to. I keep thinking I should get Randy in Sunday school, but now that I work—"

The hall door swung open and Justin rushed in, swinging a brief case in one hand, and the morning paper in another. "Good morning, ladies," he said, without really looking at either of them. He was across the reception room in two strides and on his way down the hall when he called over his shoulder, "Susie, bring your notebook. Penny, hold the calls."

Justin dictated to her all morning. It was apparent that the young attorney was getting more clients every week. After lunch, which Suzanne ate at her desk so she could study her notes, it took her all afternoon to type the letters, wills, and divorce papers he had dictated. When Penny got ready to leave for the night she looked at Suzanne sympathetically. "He really buried you today, didn't he?"

Suzanne sighed and scrunched up her shoulders. They felt as though they were on fire. She smiled. "I don't know how he has so many words stored up in that computer brain of his."

Penny covered her typewriter and locked her files. She stood up hesitantly, picked up her bag and put the strap over her shoulder, and frowned. "I hate to leave you. Hope you don't have to work too much longer."

"I think I'll be through in a few minutes. I'm on the last letter."

"Suzanne, I'd really love for you to come home with me next Tuesday night."

"Next Tuesday?"

"You know, the sharing night."

"Oh. Oh, sure. I will if I don't have any crises at home."

"Well, goodnight."

The door had just clicked shut after Penny when Justin came into the room. He walked over to Suzanne's desk and sat on the corner of it. Suzanne stopped typing and looked up at him.

After a long moment he said, "You're prettier than you were when you started." His eyes, under half-closed lids, studied her. Her cheeks got red, and she felt disturbed and pleased at the same time. But as he continued to appraise her openly, she felt indignant. How rude!

On the other hand, why shouldn't he stare? He was a man, and she had been trying hard to get her figure back—and it wasn't easy with Harriet there. Harriet was not only an excellent cook, but a nagger, always trying to make Suzanne eat two helpings of everything. Besides that, she didn't approve of Suzanne's exercise program. "All that jumpin' and situps and knee-bends will get your back out, mind my words." And so it was gratifying to think the dieting and exercise was noticeable.

However, she looked at Justin coldly, and didn't comment. Instead, she pointed at the stack on her desk. "All those need either your signature, or okay before mailing." She put her fingers on the keyboard and tried to find her place in the shorthand notebook. She felt his hot hand on her shoulder and whirled around to face him. His mouth was only inches from hers, his lips slightly open. *Oh, no! He's going to kiss me*. He looked at her mouth for a moment, and then, instead of kissing her, he stood up and lazily crossed the reception room, locked the front door, and turned toward her. His face was flushed, and his voice low as he walked back to the desk. His eyes looked hot, and his lips glistened. "You can finish that letter tomorrow."

CHAPTER 3

For a moment Suzanne panicked as Justin walked slowly toward her, his eyes locked on hers. She was trapped. She forced herself to remain calm, and tried her best to look aloof as she went back to her typing. *I'm not a child,* she thought. *If he touches me, I'll really let him have it. Of course, if I do, I'll lose my job.* She took a deep breath. Her only hope was to kid him out of this mood.

He handed her the typewriter cover. "Put it away, Susie." His voice was throaty. "I told you. It can wait until tomorrow."

"Why, Mister Wheatley!" She stared up at him in mock amazement, and dropped the cover on the floor. "Whatever do you mean, sir? You told me yourself this stuff had to get out today." She turned back to the typewriter.

"What's the matter, Susie? Don't you find me attractive?"

"Of course," she said, trying to smile without her mouth quivering. "You're very attractive, Justin, but my children—"

He pulled her to her feet and drew her close. His grip was ironlike, so tight she couldn't breathe.

"Justin!" she rasped, pushing on his chest with clenched fists. "What is the matter with you?" She squirmed free, out of breath and angry. "I can't understand why you're acting this way. You know I'm married."

"Come off it." He held her left hand up to her face. "You're not wearing rings. You haven't worn them for weeks." He pulled her roughly to his chest. "And that means one thing, you're back in circulation."

She turned her head and sighed deeply. What could she say? He had it all worked out, and it almost sounded good. For a long time, even before Del left her, she had missed being loved, being important to someone. Here was her chance, if she wanted to take it. She looked up into his green eyes, a mirror of her own. He was Hollywood-handsome, intelligent, owned his own flourishing business, had a sense of humor, and most of all, he wanted her.

Her silence seemed to encourage him and he reached out for her hand. "Why don't you relax?" he whispered. "We'd make a good team."

The rattle of the doorknob startled them apart. From the hall a voice called, "Hey, Justin. I know you're in there. Let me in."

Justin cursed. "It's Marino." He straightened his tie and buttoned his coat on the way to the door. Suzanne grabbed her purse and fled to the rest room. Her heartbeat sounded in her ears as she stared at herself in the mirror. Vincent! Her emerald eyes sparkled, and although her face was pale, and all her lipstick gone, she looked radiant. She ran a comb through her hair, touched her lips with gloss, then walked toward her office.

Vincent and Justin were seated on a couch in the reception room, looking at a blueprint. When she stepped from the hallway, both men looked up, and

51

Vincent sprang to his feet. "Suzanne!" He took a step toward her. His eyes were wide and admiring. "You look fantastic."

She smiled and walked hesitantly toward him. In the center of the room she shyly offered her hand, and he took it between hot, dry palms. As she looked up into his dark eyes she experienced that now familiar sinking sensation, and automatically put a hand to her breast.

"How is your daughter?" she stammered, smiling so hard she could feel it in her cheeks.

"Fine, fine." He beamed down at her and held on to her hand. "How're your children?"

"Just fine." She couldn't look away. As they gazed at each other, it seemed as though they were caught in a shimmering bubble, a rainbow world of their own.

But Justin, now all business and rather peevish, broke the spell. "These plans look great to me, Vincent. But you know you can't break ground, yet."

Vincent gave her hand an extra squeeze then let her go as he turned to look at Justin. "I know. But I thought maybe you could put the screws on somebody."

Justin raised his hands irritably. "I'm doing all I can do. It takes time." He scowled at Suzanne.

Vincent nodded. "I know that. Actually, the real reason I came by tonight was because I wanted to ask this young lady out to dinner." His eyes, as he turned to look at Suzanne, were as soft as brown velvet.

Justin's face became expressionless. After a moment he said, "Well, you almost missed us. We were just closing up."

Suzanne, smiling, went to her desk and sat down with her back to them. She covered the typewriter, then locked the desk drawer. When she picked up her purse Justin said, "Aren't you going to finish that letter?"

Suzanne stared at him, unblinking. "You told me it could wait until tomorrow, didn't you?"

His mouth tightened and he drew in his breath and let it out with a snort.

"How about it, Suzanne?" Vincent asked, apparently unaware of Justin's aggravation. "Dinner with a lonesome old widower?"

"I couldn't go tonight, Vincent. I've made other plans." She bit her lip as she looked into his eyes. For a moment she almost decided to go with him, but she thought of the long list of groceries she had to buy.

He frowned and shook his head sadly. "And to think I risked my neck on the Golden State freeway this afternoon, trying to get to you before you went home."

"I'm sorry," Suzanne said, meaning it with all her heart. "But I just can't tonight."

"She's a family woman," Justin said sarcastically. "Didn't you know? Even I tried to get her companionship this evening."

Vincent's smile faded, as he turned slowly to look at Justin, then back at her. *No, no, Vincent,* she wanted to scream. *There's nothing between us!* "My children are waiting," she said aloud, "and my mother-in-law is counting on me to buy groceries." She lifted her chin. "But, some other time?" She looked at him wistfully.

He opened his mouth as though to argue, but evidently thought better of it. He shrugged, then his eyes brightened. "Tomorrow, then, okay? I'll take you to lunch. I'll be here just before noon. All right?" Suzanne nodded and flashed a brilliant smile. He looked over at Justin. "And don't worry, Counselor. I'll bring her back at one o'clock, sharp."

Suzanne put the strap of her bag over her shoulder and crossed the room. "Goodnight," she called, her anger at Justin had abated with the pleasure of being near Vincent. "I'll look forward to lunch tomorrow."

Justin was not in the office the next morning, and she was relieved. She hoped he understood her position, and would not make any more advances. And she had lunch with Vincent to think about. The butterflies in her stomach increased with each minute. She had had a terrible time deciding what to wear to work, and promised herself that when she got her next paycheck she would buy a new dress. After pulling almost everything she owned out of the closet, she finally chose her old black, pinstripe skirt and a soft white blouse.

"Don't you look pretty," Penny remarked at work. "Somebody went shopping last night."

"Oh, no. This outfit is old, old."

"Sure doesn't look it. It's right in style."

"My mother told me that black and white are always in style," Suzanne answered, then motioned toward the hall. "Has our boss come in?"

"No, remember? He's in court this morning."

Suzanne's eyes closed with relief. "Oh, that's right." Thank heaven I don't have to face him this morning.

"Why? Didn't you get all your transcribing done last night?"

Suzanne looked at Penny and decided not to mention Justin's behavior. She shook her head and smiled wryly. "No, I didn't! I have three more letters to type." She opened her desk, pulled up the typewriter, and uncovered it. "Maybe I can get caught up while he's gone. I still have billing to do, too."

"It'll be easier when the new computer comes."

Suzanne looked doubtful. "I just hope I can learn how to use it." She opened the steno pad and studied her cold notes. "When's it supposed to be here?"

"What?" Penny's sapphire eyes were blank.

"The computer."

"Oh. Any day, I think," Penny answered. "The salesman had to order special discs for a law office. I think that's what's holding it up."

Suzanne turned to the typewriter and began to transcribe. She raced with the morning hours, trying to get all her work done so Justin couldn't find fault. She had a growing, uneasy feeling that he might look for trouble since he didn't get his way with her last night. She wanted this job. It was nice to be earning money. But she knew he was angry with her, and her future could be shaky. Of course she could always claim harassment, but what a sticky mess that would be. Why had he spoiled it all? Now she could never feel at ease with him again. Men!

As she was arranging letters for him to sign, Justin burst through the door. He looked pleasant and businesslike as he breezed through the reception room. "Susie, grab your pen. We've got work to do."

Suzanne looked at her watch. Eleven-forty-five! "Oh no!" she whispered and glanced at Penny. "I've got a lunch date with Vincent Marino."

Penny's eyes widened. "No kidding! What time?"

"He'll be here any moment. What'll I do, Penny?" Her voice was a wail.

"Just tell him. Tell Mr. Wheatley you have a date."

Suzanne's full lips tightened. "He knows I have this date. He was here when Vincent came last night." She picked up her notebook and pen, and sighing, started out the gate. She looked back. "Please tell Vincent," she felt a lump in her throat, "I'm so sorry." At Penny's stricken look she added, "I just can't force the issue. I need this job."

Inside Justin's office she sat primly on the edge of a chair, notebook opened, pen poised.

"Susie." His voice was low. She looked up at him, her face as expressionless as she could make it. He looked up at her from under frowning eyebrows. His face was sad. "Susie, I'm very ashamed of myself. If you can, please forgive how rotten I was."

Relief washed over her like a warm bath. She looked directly into his eyes and smiled. She swallowed, then whispered, "Forgotten."

Immediately he became his buoyant self. "Now I know you have a lunch date with Mr. Important Client, so you'd better touch up your makeup." He tapped a drumbeat with a yellow pencil while he grinned at her. Unbelieving, Suzanne slowly got to her feet. "And if you can't make it in an hour," he winked and grinned, "take an extra five minutes."

Vincent was just walking into the office when Suzanne came out of the rest room. She beamed at him. "I'll get my bag and be right with you."

As they walked up to the door of an obscure little restaurant, Vincent remarked, "This place doesn't look like much on the outside, but it's the one place I know where we can order, and be out in an hour." He opened the door for her. "And the food's terrific."

It was so dark inside Suzanne stopped short. Instinctively, she reached for him. He tucked her hand in his arm, and held her securely while they waited for the hostess. Her heartbeat increased, and she felt breathless. After they were seated in a back booth, she could barely make out a bar and several red-checked tables. The menu prices were outrageous. She hated to order a meal, because she knew she was too excited to eat. Although there was at least a foot of space between them, she could almost feel his warmth and vitality, and she felt a hypnotic pull toward him. It was all she could do to sit quietly in the booth and study the menu. She longed to touch him. She even wondered how far apart their feet were under the table.

"What will you have, little Suzanne?"

The waitress approached. "Something from the bar?" she asked.

Vincent looked inquiringly at Suzanne and she shook her head. He smiled at the waitress and said, "We'll pass."

In spite of his protests, Suzanne again ordered soup, and as before, he ordered steak. After they had ordered, Vincent faced her, tilted his head, and stared at her, first at her hair, then her lips, and finally into her eyes. She thought he had the deepest, most beautiful eyes she had ever looked into.

"Suzanne, I have to tell you, I've been thinking about you a lot."

She bit her lip, then smiled shyly. "What kind of thoughts do you think about me?" Her voice was a little more than a whisper.

"Thoughts like I want to know everything about you. The first thing," he took her hand, "are you married or not?" Her smile disappeared, and she looked away. "You don't have to tell me," he spoke quickly. "It's just that the first time we had lunch you were wearing rings." He lifted her fingers almost to his lips. "And now you aren't."

She looked into his eyes, and again experienced a thrill that swept from her heart through her body, leaving her weak. She took a breath. "Vincent, I'm in the process of getting, of being divorced."

His black brows raised. "He's divorcing you?"

She nodded. "He wanted me to file, but I'm against divorce, so he went ahead with it."

She stopped talking when the waitress brought their food. When she was gone Vincent said, "It's none of my business, of course. And don't answer if you don't want to. But why? Why is he divorcing you?"

"He doesn't love me anymore. And he loves someone else." It had been almost four months since Del left, but it still hurt to admit he loved another woman.

"Then on what grounds could he divorce you?"

"It's easy in California. 'Irreconcilable differences.'" She watched him cut into his steak and put a bite in his mouth. He looked stern and she wondered if it would make a difference in how he felt, now that he knew Del had rejected her? She picked up her soup spoon and slowly stirred the hot broth. "I could have gotten the divorce," she explained, "but I didn't want it. I've always believed that divorce is wrong." She realized she was trying to justify her position, and felt ashamed, then frustrated. Why did she have to feel ashamed? None of this was her fault . . . was it?

He looked at her and nodded slightly with a trace of a smile on his lips. He reached out as though to pat her, but dropped his hand. "Do you want to tell me about it, or does it distress you?"

She shrugged and lifted her palms. "There's not much to tell. Del and I were married in my second year of college, I worked for awhile, then we had Randy."

"Was it a happy marriage?"

"Yes. At least, I thought it was. I was content."

"But were you in love?"

Suzanne glanced quickly at him and then down at her soup. "Of course." Had she loved Del? Yes—but there had never been any of the wild excitement going on inside as there always was with this man. Every time she looked at him it was like going down on an elevator. She forced herself to swallow a spoonful of soup.

"Then what happened?"

"I really don't know. After his company transferred him to Los Angeles he began to drink quite a bit. He said he had to, because of business. He had to be out of town a lot, too."

"Drinking and business trips can hurt any marriage."

"But I'm sure it wasn't all his fault. After Randy was born I'm afraid I was probably more mother than wife. I've read articles about that. I was so happy with my baby, I may have made him feel left out. And when Crystal came. . . ," she shook her head. "She threw all our schedules out the window. There wasn't any time for anyone but Crystal." She laughed shortly. "My mother-in-law says she's spoiled."

58

"Tell me about it," Vincent said, suddenly laughing. His white teeth flashed in the dim light. "It's impossible not to spoil a daughter." He finished his steak and wiped his lips with a napkin. "Well, my dear Suzanne, I don't believe in divorce, either. I know in our church it's a sin—but then, there are many sins. Who's to say whether divorce is a bigger sin than lying, or eating too much?"

"What church do you go to?"

"I haven't been inside a church since my wife's funeral."

Suzanne noted bitterness in his voice, and felt a twinge of jealousy. He probably still missed her a great deal; she had only been dead three years. "Tell me about her," she said softly.

He sighed deeply, and with his elbows on the table, hands laced, he leaned forward and blew gently on his thumbs. After a long pause he said, "She was tiny and dark, and her movements were quick, like a little bird." He smiled sadly at Suzanne. "She was so alive. She seemed to be everywhere at once. She did everything—made clothes for herself and Carla, gardened, cooked, and loved me." He shook his head. "She was a dynamo. I couldn't believe it when she told me she was sick, and even now sometimes, I can't believe she's gone."

Suzanne looked at his profile, handsome, yet his expression was sad. *He'll probably never forget her.*

But suddenly he turned to face her, and put his hands, large and warm, on her cheeks. "Suzanne, we've spent our whole lunch hour in the past. From now on, let's forget it. Let's enjoy what we have today."

She searched his eyes for truth, then reached up and touched one of his hands. Without warning he kissed her on the mouth, a long, warm, soft kiss.

CHAPTER 6

SEVERAL TIMES THROUGH the afternoon hours, Suzanne closed her eyes and touched her lips with her fingertips. Each time she relived that tender kiss, a fire-and-ice sensation shimmered through her body. She smiled as she remembered how his eyes had widened when he pulled away from her. He had let out his breath in a low whistle and whispered, "Time to get you back to the office." During the short drive back he made a real date with her. He was going to take her to dinner Saturday night on the grand old luxury liner, the Queen Mary, now permanently berthed at Long Beach.

When Suzanne awoke Saturday morning she pulled on old jeans and a faded blue tee shirt and hurried, barefoot, into the kitchen. She had a million things to do. Harriet always went to her own apartment for the weekend. "My plants need me," she explained. But Suzanne was sure it was also to recuperate from the back-aching job of taking care of Crystal. Whatever the reason, she was grateful. Saturdays and Sundays meant everything to her. Over the past couple of months she had come to love Harriet sincerely. She was so good to all of them, but Suzanne needed time alone, and she needed time with the children without Harriet's supervision.

It had begun to bother Suzanne the way authority had changed hands. When she told the children to do something, they always looked at Harriet for confirmation. Of course, Harriet always backed her up. "Mind Mommy," she'd say. But she wondered if Harriet said, "No, you don't have to do that," who they would obey. She wished someone else could watch the children, but she couldn't imagine "firing" Harriet.

But her mind wasn't on Harriet or the children this morning. Her mind and heart were with Vincent. Could it be possible? Tonight she had a real date with him! She planned to wear her green silk dress. It was two years old, but just the other day she had seen one almost like it in an expensive shop in the mall. It had ruffles around the neck and wrists, and the shade of green exactly matched her eyes. She had been diligent about regaining her figure, and had succeeded. It was wonderful to feel slender again.

"I'm hungry, Mom." Suzanne turned to see Randy standing in the kitchen door, holding his grubby Snoopy dog. *His pajamas are getting too little,* she thought. *Every payday something extra!* He came to her and leaned against the cupboard. "Are we going to have pancakes?"

"Do you want pancakes? I was going to cook oatmeal."

"Yuk. Can't we have pancakes?" He was beside her now, looking up with round eyes.

"Okay. But you have to eat an orange first, and I want you to drink a full glass of milk, too."

"Before the pancakes?"

"Not the milk. With them."

"Grandma makes hot chocolate."

"Well, I don't! You don't need chocolate in your stomach. It's like so much mud."

"But Grandma—"

"Randy, that's enough. Isn't that Crystal? Go see if she's awake, please."

Her chores consumed the day. Mechanically, she made pancakes, fed and dressed Crystal, did six loads of laundry, helped Randy bury a dead sparrow, wrestled Crystal into the car seat, raced to the market, put gas in the car, fixed lunch, pressed clothes, bathed Crystal, rocked her at naptime, and argued with Randy after his shower because his neck wasn't clean.

At last it was five-thirty and time for her own shower.

"Now if only Cheryl will be on time," she said aloud.

"Is she baby-sitting us?" Randy asked.

"Mmm hmm. Remember, I told you I was going out to dinner tonight?"

"Why can't we go, too?"

"This man doesn't know you yet. Maybe another time, after he meets you, we can all go somewhere together."

"Is he a friend of daddy's?"

Suzanne was relieved when the doorbell sounded. She hurried to open the door and stood aside. "Hi, Cheryl!" Selena's daughter, a slender, dark-eyed teenage girl stepped in. "I'm so glad you could come."

Cheryl wore skintight jeans and a pink top. Her straight, almost black hair was below her shoulders, and swept back from her forehead. She was smiling, and her lips glistened with pink gloss. Her eye makeup was a three-color masterpiece. "Am I late? Mom said you wanted me early so you could get ready."

"No, honey, you're not late, but now that you're here, I'll go shower."

As she shampooed her hair she wondered what would become of Cheryl in the years ahead. She was eighteen, and had already been engaged twice. Now she was going to college, but Selena said, "She's playing. All she's looking for is a good time. I pray to the saints she won't get pregnant." A vague uneasiness took away some of the excitement of her date with Vincent. She hoped Cheryl wouldn't have a fellow over here tonight.

She waved away the thought with the hair dryer, blowing her copper colored hair around her face. Still, the anxious feeling persisted. Why was she worrying? Hadn't she known Cheryl since she was little? She had kept the children many times, and they loved her. Anyway, Selena was just next door. Everything would be all right. Suddenly, Penny's face, with her eyes closed in prayer, appeared in her mind. Suzanne stared at her frowning self in the mirror. *I wish I could pray like that. Penny prays about everything.* She put down the dryer and tossed the brush in a drawer. *Am I being morbid, or what?*

With quick, determined movements she began to apply her makeup. She used more eyeshadow than usual and was pleased with the effect. Her hair turned out with just the right amount of curl, and when she put on the green dress and high heeled black sandals she felt good about herself. She took stock of her perfumes—not that she had a great supply—but perfumes had to be special to her, or she wouldn't wear them. She held a spray bottle of *Tigress* in her hand, her favorite for years, but she doubted she would wear it anymore. It brought back the past with Del. She touched a bottle of *Bouquet*. She loved the scent when she was pregnant, but now she couldn't stand it.

She picked up a tiny bottle of a new perfume that had been a gift. She touched the applicator to her wrists, then her ear lobes. She breathed deeply and smiled. It's scent was perfect for a night at the ocean, an evening on the luxurious Queen Mary.

She smiled at her image, "A new perfume for a new love."

The doorbell rang. "I'll get it!" she called to Cheryl. She snatched up her purse and a black sweater, then hurried to the front door.

Suzanne's lips parted and she drew in her breath when she saw Vincent. He looked magnificent in a dark blue suit, white shirt, and tie. But it was the look in his eyes when he saw her that made her breath catch. It was the look of love.

"Come in." Her voice was almost a whisper. His bulk filled the doorway as he stepped inside the living room. As he brushed by her she smelled his shaving lotion, and felt the warmth of his body. "These are my children," she said in a normal voice. "The lovely young lady is my next door neighbor, Cheryl."

Cheryl glanced up from her magazine. "Hi."

"And my son. Randy, come shake hands with Mr. Marino."

Reluctantly, Randy put down a piece of his Star Wars set, pursed his lips to one side, and walked slowly toward Vincent.

"Hi, fella. Playing Star Wars?"

Randy nodded silently, without smiling.

"I don't blame you," Vincent spoke easily. "I saw the picture twice myself."

Randy eyed him, then smiled on one side of his mouth. "Wasn't it neat?" His round, dark eyes glowed. "Would you take me again, sometime?"

"Randy." Suzanne frowned a warning.

"Sure I'll take you, if your mother'll let me."

"How about tonight?"

Vincent cleared his throat and smiled at Suzanne. "Well, I don't believe we can make it tonight, son. Your mother and I have reservations on the—we have reservations for dinner."

"Do you know my daddy?"

"Randy, we have to be going now. Come here, Crystal, and tell Mommy bye-bye."

In another moment or two they walked down the front sidewalk and Suzanne waited for Vincent to open the car door.

"You didn't drive your Porsche tonight," she observed. She looked at the heavy, black and chrome car. "Is this a Cadillac?"

"An old one."

Suzanne sank into the soft black leather seat and smiled up at Vincent as he closed the door. In a moment he swung in under the wheel, and Suzanne was acutely aware of his nearness. Her heartbeat quickened and her mouth felt dry. She longed to snuggle up to him but primly forced herself a few inches toward the right side of the car. But she couldn't take her eyes away from his profile as the car glided away from the curbing.

"Have you ever been on the Queen Mary?" he asked as he turned on Hacienda Boulevard toward the freeway.

"Yes, when we first moved here, several years ago, but at that time there wasn't too much open to the public. We saw the engine room, but I don't believe there were any restaurants on board—at least we didn't eat anything."

"We're going to eat at the Sir Winston. I think you'll like it."

"I know I will."

They rode several miles without talking, enjoying soft music on the stereo, and watching the red clouds of sunset turn to purple, then dark blue. Suzanne wanted to tell him how happy she was to be with him, but an inborn shyness kept her from speaking. *If I ever start talking,* she thought, *I'll tell him I love him, and I must not be so stupid, so crazy.* As the silence between them lengthened she groped for something to say. "Have you gotten any more evidence for your case?"

Vincent straightened. "No." There was another lapse, and then, "Suzanne, let's not talk about business tonight. I want to talk about you, about us." He reached out for her hand, lifted it to his lips and kissed her icy fingers. "You're cold, come over."

She moved slightly toward him and he pulled his arm around her shoulder. Gently, firmly, he pulled her close. "Little Suzanne. I've looked forward to this night for a long time."

"A long time?" her voice teased. "We just made the date a couple of days ago."

"I know, but since our first lunch together I've thought about having you to myself." He changed lanes and made a long, looping curve to the Long Beach freeway. "You probably won't believe this, but you're the first woman I've been excited about since Madge died."

Suzanne did not respond, but he must have read her thoughts. "Yes, there have been other women, but they were only time fillers, to get through the long weekends when I couldn't work."

She looked out the windshield at the thousands of red taillights ahead of them. It seemed the whole world was moving toward Long Beach. "I know what it is to be lonely."

"Isn't it strange," he said as he pulled her closer, "even with a house full of people, you can still be lonely." She closed her eyes and nodded. "At my house, my daughter Carla usually has friends in, you know, the kind that laugh like billy goats, and eat like hogs. And then Kristen is usually kicking up a fuss."

"Kristen?" She turned to look at him.

"My granddaughter." His mouth tightened. "She's Carla's three-year-old daughter."

"Oh, yes. I remember, from the will."

Silence filled the car, as heavy as the Cadillac itself.

At last he sighed and took his arm away from Suzanne's shoulder. "Well, there she is, the Queen Mary. Did you know it cost four million dollars to restore her to glory?"

The great ship loomed out of the darkness, powerful-looking and regal. She was decorated with garlands of lights across her top, which illuminated her three huge stacks.

The parking area seemed almost to have a carnival atmosphere, thought Suzanne, as people got out of their cars laughing and talking, on their way to the elevators.

"How tall and slender she is," Vincent murmured, almost to himself. He leaned back, staring up. "Makes you wonder what kept her from rolling over on the high seas."

Instinctively, as Suzanne took in the mammoth ship, she slipped her arm through Vincent's and felt his arm tighten on hers. A uniformed attendant, with sober British dignity, directed them to the Sir Winston.

When they stepped out of the elevator onto the deck, Suzanne said, "Just think! We're walking on the very boards where the famous movie stars have strolled."

"But none were more lovely than you, Suzanne." Vincent's voice and expression were so solemn, Suzanne had to laugh. "No! I mean it." He turned her to face him. "My darling, you must know how I feel. I love you."

Suzanne's legs suddenly felt weak and her heart pounded. Could this be happening? Could he really be so attracted to her? Granted, her own feelings for him were sweet and wondrous, but never in her wildest dreams did she feel anyone would ever return her love again. "Please, Vincent. I feel lightheaded. Could we sit down?"

"Of course. But we're almost at the restaurant, can you make it?"

The rest of the evening was a blur of tuxedos, candlelight, and fairytale happiness. Whenever she gazed into his eyes, she felt the delicious elevator sensation inside and hoped the magical evening would go on forever. She was losing her heart to this wonderful man, and yet in the back of her mind was some unnamed worry, some fretting that threatened her acceptance of the possibility before her.

After the meal he took her arm and suggested a stroll around the deck. Remarkably, talk through the evening had not yet centered on their children. Now Vincent turned to her with a suggestion.

"How would you like to bring Randy and Crystal to my place next Sunday? I'd like to get acquainted with them. Randy could play in the pool, and there's plenty of room to run around. Kristen's too young for him, but she's got every gadget on the market."

Suzanne laughed. "What a granddad!"

"Will you come?"

"All right, Vincent," she said.

"Oh, that's wonderful. I'm anxious for you to meet Carla and Kristen, too. If it's warm enough I'll have Nell serve lunch by the pool, be sure to bring your suit." He took her hand. "And if it's cold, we'll build a fire in the fireplace, turn the kids loose in the recreation room, and. . . ." His eyes narrowed as he looked into hers. He touched her lips with his finger, then traced her cheek, brushed back a few tendrils of hair, then kissed her lightly on the cheek. He whispered in her ear, "I love you, Suzanne, and I want you for my wife."

The words were as real as the love in his eyes. And how she wanted to love him in return! She took his hand quietly and lifted it to her cheek, but the tears misting her eyes were not from joy.

CHAPTER 7

"DID YOU HEAR me?" He touched her chin to make her look up at him.

"Yes, I heard you." She gazed into his eyes for a moment, then looked down. "I don't know what to say."

"I know you care for me."

"Yes."

"Then?"

She walked slowly, matching his steps. "For one thing, Vincent, my divorce isn't final." She studied his face. "Besides, isn't it against your religion to marry a divorced person?"

He waved his hand and frowned. "I told you I never go to church. I think all of those dos and don'ts are manmade to make us feel guilty."

She stared out at the lights of Long Beach for a moment, then looked up at him. "I don't know much about religion, although my mother took me to church when I was little, but I do know there's some place in the Bible that says divorced people shouldn't re-marry."

He shrugged. "That's true." They walked for a while in silence.

"Oh, Vincent," she said with a squeeze of his arm, "I'm looking forward to meeting your daughter, and Kristen, too. Do you think they'll like me? And Randy and Crystal?"

"How could anyone not like you?" He looked away briefly, and Suzanne thought his shoulders drooped a little. When he looked at her again, however, he smiled. "Of course they'll like you."

But a chilling premonition again descended on Suzanne. She shivered.

Vincent looked into her eyes, then kissed her cheek. "So, when can we be married?"

"Oh, you!" She pretended intense interest in the narrow boards of the deck. At last she looked up at him. "Please don't be offended at what I'm going to say, okay?" He flicked a glance at her, but didn't comment. They walked silently for a few moments, both looking straight ahead. "I really care for you," she began. "At least, I think I do. But so many things have happened to me in such a short time, I'm not sure how I feel." His arm slid from her waist and she looked up. "I don't see how you can be sure of your feelings either, Vincent. It's too soon."

"Not for me. I always know what I want." His manner was brusque. "I know I want you, but evidently, the feeling isn't mutual."

"I didn't say that! Please, give me a little time. You don't even know me or my kids. In a few weeks you might hate us!"

He snorted, then put his arm around her again. She leaned into him, and could feel his thigh against hers as they walked.

They wandered about, looking at the magnificent ship, yet Suzanne wasn't really seeing anything. She was stunned at the depth of her emotion. Even when she was first in love with Del she had never felt as she

70

did now. As her heart began to beat more normally, she tried to find something to say.

"I've always thought it would be wonderful to go on a cruise."

"Marry me, and we'll go."

"Vincent!" She laughed, walking quickly and pulling him along, "I think we better go home."

He was beside her in an instant. "Okay, Missey. I'll not bother you anymore now. But I'll expect an answer next weekend."

He kept his word on the way home, not even offering to put his arm around her. Suzanne ached to sit close to him, but made herself stay in the right corner. What she had told him was true. It was too soon.

As on the way to the Queen, she drank in his profile in the light of oncoming freeway traffic. She couldn't seem to get enough of looking at him. His head was well-shaped, and she liked the length of his hair. Not long, but not clipped short, either. As he concentrated on driving, his brows came together and his eyes narrowed, making him seem even more handsome to Suzanne. He glanced at her and smiled. "You okay?"

"Of course."

"The way you were staring at me, I thought maybe something was wrong."

She felt color rise in her cheeks. "I'm sorry. I was just wondering about you."

"What would you like to know about me?"

"How did you get started building condominiums?"

"My dad was building houses before I was born, so I grew up in the construction business. All my summers were spent working for him. By the time I was eighteen I could run a job."

"You mean at eighteen you were the boss?"

He winked at her and shrugged. "Under his license, of course. But by that time he'd taught me how to estimate costs, how to bid, how to order materials,

71

and build. I loved it then, and thought I was quite a hotshot, but he wanted me to go to college and get a degree. Things were getting more complicated, and he felt I needed a lot more knowledge to compete in the building game than he could give me. So after high school I went to U.C.L.A. for two years." He sighed, and lifted his hand from the wheel. "Then he had a heart attack, and within four days he was gone."

He accelerated and moved into the fast lane, passed a slow-moving car, then drifted back to the middle lane. "After two years in college I wasn't sure if I wanted to be a contractor or not, but when Dad died, he had a couple of jobs going, and I knew he'd want me to finish them. Then more contracts began to come in, stuff he had bid on months earlier. I took the contractor's test, and decided if I passed it, I'd take over the business, and if not. . . ." He smiled, but Suzanne thought he looked sad. "By this time I was engaged to Madge, I passed the test, and we got married. From then on there's never been a place to quit."

"Don't you like construction?"

"Oh, sure. But like anything else, sometimes it gets old. And the hassles about zoning, licenses, city ordinances, all the taxes—sometimes it gets to me. But it's a good living. I shouldn't complain."

"Do you ever build houses now, or are they all condominiums?"

"I haven't built any single dwellings for a long time. Why?"

"I just wondered. I was thinking how marvelous it must be to plan your very own house, and have it exactly as you want it, you know? All the cupboards and closets."

He took her hand. "If you marry me, I'll build you a house, any way you want it." He squeezed her fingers. "I'm sorry, Suzanne. I just can't keep from pressuring you."

Suzanne allowed him to lace his fingers in hers, and closed her eyes. *I love him*, she thought, *and he loves me. What a life we could have together. The children would be financially secure, and I could quit work. Why am I fighting?*

She opened her eyes as he turned into her driveway and stopped. He looked at her but made no attempt to kiss her. He got out and walked quickly around to her side of the car and opened the door. "It's only ten o'clock."

"That is early," she answered. "Would you like some coffee?"

"Milk and cookies would be better." He helped her out of the car, and they walked toward the front door.

"Milk and cookies, huh?" She laughed softly. "Well, I know there's milk, and Harriet made oatmeal cookies yesterday, but you know I have a growing son, and besides that, tonight a teenager has had access to the cookie jar." She handed him the front door key.

He chuckled, turned the knob, and stood aside for her to enter.

A sickening smell filled her nostrils. She looked around quickly for Cheryl, but she wasn't in sight.

"Smells like your baby sitter has been sampling more than cookies."

"Cheryl?" Suzanne ran to the kitchen, and Vincent followed. Cheryl wasn't there. She frowned and bit her lip. "Where is she? Oh, my, the children!" She ran across the linoleum and down the hall to Crystal's room. The baby was standing in her crib, smiling and shaking the rail. "Baby! Oh, my baby. Mommy's home." Suzanne swooped her up. "Yuk! You're dripping wet." She threw a blanket around the baby, then holding her tightly, she ran the few steps down the hall to Randy's room. He was asleep, uncovered, with his knees drawn up to his chin.

"Thank God he's safe," she breathed.

"Ranny safe," Crystal mimicked, and pointed at her brother.

Vincent stepped in front of Suzanne, pulled the sheet and blanket up around Randy's shoulders, and tucked them in. Automatically, he patted the boy.

Together, they went back to the nursery, and in spite of Crystal's determined effort to get away, Suzanne unsnapped her sleepers. "Here's the reason she's wet. Look how Cheryl put this diaper on!" She tossed the wet clothes in the hamper, then washed and powdered the baby. "Where is that girl?"

Vincent stepped out in the hall. In a moment he was beside Suzanne. "She's not in the bathroom."

Suzanne closed her eyes for an instant and shook her head. She dressed Crystal, then picked her up. "I don't know what to think. I've had her baby-sit a lot of times." She sniffed the air, and made a face. "Nothing like this ever happened before. Maybe she went home for a minute."

"Smoking pot's against the law. You can't allow yourself to be jeopardized."

They both froze when they heard a door open. They looked at each other, then stepped out into the hall.

Cheryl was coming out of Suzanne's bedroom, her long hair tangled, her makeup gone. Her eyes were bloodshot.

"Oh, hi." She giggled. "Wow. You're home early." Her voice was shrill. "Uh oh." She smiled and turned back toward the bedroom. "Excuse me."

"She's high," Vincent whispered.

Suzanne's heart began to beat in her throat, and she felt as she had so many nights in the past, when Del had come home drunk. Always, the sight of him, when he wasn't in his right mind, had frightened her, and filled her with disgust.

They watched Cheryl go back into the bedroom.

Suzanne's mouth opened. "She has no business in my room."

In a second Cheryl returned, smoothing her hair and smiling apologetically.

"Cheryl, what's going on?"

Cheryl's smile quivered. She glanced at Vincent, then back at Suzanne. "Stan, you know, my boyfriend, came over. He got sick so I told him he could rest in your room."

Suzanne's eyes flashed at Vincent. She could feel her mouth draw down at the corners. "Well, sick or not, I want you to tell him to leave."

"Okay. Okay." Cheryl turned meekly and disappeared behind the bedroom door.

Vincent put his arm around Suzanne and steered her toward the living room. They sat down on the couch and Crystal beamed at Vincent. She put chubby hands over her eyes again, then peeked at him. "Boo!"

Vincent laughed. "Boo, yourself."

When Cheryl and her boyfriend crossed the room, without looking in their direction, Suzanne couldn't help feeling sorry for him. How embarrassed he must feel. They both went outside, but in less than a minute Cheryl came back in, hugging herself. "It's really cold tonight," she said. She sat down opposite them. "I'm sorry, Suzanne." She didn't look sorry.

Suzanne was breathless with anger. "I'm disappointed in you, Cheryl. I never thought you'd have a man over here without my permission, much less smoke marijuana in my home. You were supposed to be taking care of the children."

Cheryl looked sullen. "Are you going to tell Mom?"

"Yes. I have to. And I won't trouble you to keep the children again." She put Crystal on the floor. "Excuse me a minute and I'll get your money."

"Money?" she echoed.

"For baby-sitting."

"Oh."

"Here, let me get it." Vincent stood up and reached for his billfold, and pulled out a bill.

Cheryl took it, then looked around the room. "What'd I do with my bag? Oh, there it is. Well, guess I'd better go." She opened the front door, waved and smiled. "Bye."

Crystal waved and called, "Bye, bye."

Suzanne sank down on the couch, and shook her head.

Vincent sniffed and frowned. "Whew. Sorry to tell you this, lady, but your house stinks." He opened the front door and fanned it back and forth.

"I still can't believe it. She acted so, so casual. And it certainly messes up any future dates I might make with you."

"Why?"

"She's the only baby-sitter I know."

"How about your mother-in-law?"

Suzanne raised an eyebrow at him. "Ask Harriet to baby-sit, while I go out with someone besides her son?"

"Oh, well. We'll find someone. Anyway, you won't need a sitter next weekend." He leaned over and picked up Crystal. "Isn't she a doll? Just like her mother." He kissed her on the cheek. "Yes sir. Next week Crystal's going to meet her new family."

CHAPTER 8

SUZANNE COULDN'T WAIT to go to the office on Monday morning. In spite of Crystal's demands, Randy's incessant talking, and endless weekend chores, Sunday had been long and empty. She thought of Vincent almost constantly. Many times that day she closed her eyes and tried to remember every word he had said, and how his lips felt on hers.

Why had she told him she couldn't see him Sunday? Was it because she felt guilty for not spending more time with the children? Probably. But he seemed to really enjoy them. She smiled as she remembered how he'd tucked the blanket up around Randy's shoulders. They could have had a good time together yesterday. She'd been on the verge of calling him several times, but her mother had taught her, "Never call a man; let him call you." The phone had rung twice, her heart had leaped, but it was only Randy's friend Jimmy. What did she expect? She had told him firmly she would be busy with the children and household duties. No wonder he hadn't called.

Maybe he'll call today, she thought, as she unlocked the office door. Looking both feminine and efficient in a new pink blouse with white collar and cuffs, she went into Justin's office, sharpened his pencils, laid out legal pads, and turned his calendar. He was usually in court on Mondays, for which she was thankful. It gave her a chance to collect herself, and get ready for his whirlwind approach to work.

She went to the rest room, combed her hair, then put water in a cracked vase, went back to Justin's office and poured it on his potted palm and nephthytis. In spite of his warning that watering plants wasn't in her job description, she had assumed this chore ever since she had come in one morning and found the nephthytis drooping almost to the floor. "Why don't you just throw them out?" he had growled. "I can't remember to water the dumb things." But Suzanne had assured him it was no problem to water them once a week. "I love plants. I've got lots of them at home." Now she had lots of them at work, in the reception room and on top of the file cabinet.

As she sat down at her desk and uncovered the typewriter, her mind ran again to Vincent. Maybe he would have some reason to come in. She closed her eyes and recalled his face; his burning eyes, his warm lips. Her desire to see him was almost a passion. She opened her steno pad and stared at the notes, cold and meaningless. She read some of the attached correspondence, but it seemed almost impossible to get her mind on work.

Penny burst through the front door, radiant as usual, wearing a summery dress with a full skirt and lace around the neck. "Good morning," she bubbled. "Isn't it a super day? The sun's shining!"

Suzanne looked up and smiled. "For a change. I've never gotten used to L.A. gray mornings." She turned back to her work. "In Colorado the sun shines almost every day."

"The wind was really zipping around yesterday.

That's why it's so beautiful this morning." Penny dropped an oversized, overstuffed bag on her desk and sprawled in her chair. "Man, I'm tired this morning. We had a fantastic day, yesterday, though."

"Who's we?" Suzanne's question was mechanical. Over the past several weeks she had learned to keep working as Penny talked.

"Oh, I mean at church. I remember when I was younger trying all sorts of things to make the time go fast during church, you know, holding my breath, scribbling on the bulletin." She giggled. "But our pastor is so interesting. He takes a certain chapter, then sort of explains every verse." She forced her bag in a drawer and flipped her hair out of her face. "And the choir's super. Then there's always something doing with the singles on Sunday night. Like last night, after church, we all piled in the bus and went to a Christian jazz concert."

Suzanne looked up and her eyebrow lifted. "A Christian jazz concert?"

"Yeah. The artists all love the Lord, and give their testimonies, and the music is the best." She sighed. "But I'm pooped today." She took a stack of papers out of her basket, shuffled them around, then rested her head on her hand and stared into space.

Suzanne was just beginning to make sense out of her notes when Penny interrupted.

"Suzanne, I hope you won't think I'm bugging you."

"What?" She looked up with a hint of a frown.

Penny looked apologetic. "Tomorrow's Tuesday, remember?"

"Tuesday?" Suzanne's frown deepened, and she bit her lip.

"Sharing? Tuesday night, Bible study at my house? John Dempsey?"

Suzanne let out her breath. She felt trapped and annoyed. She had no desire to listen all evening to some fellow talk about the Bible. Even listening to Harriet was better than that. She smiled politely. "Oh, I do remember you said something about that."

"Can you come? My mom cooked a fourteen pound turkey Saturday, and she made me take half of it home. We can have hot turkey sandwiches, or turkey salad, or whatever you want, so long as it's mostly turkey."

Penny's sweetness touched her. In spite of her irritation she grinned. "Sure, I'll come, but I can't stay late." She looked back at her notes. "It's a good thing you mentioned it today so I can warn my mother-in-law. I've never left her with the kids in the evening before."

She thought about Saturday night's calamity with Cheryl. If Harriet had been keeping the kids none of that would have happened.

"Well, I suppose you could bring the children." Penny's voice was soft.

"What? Oh, no. I wouldn't think of bringing them. My mother-in-law stays with me through the week. I'll ask her."

"Maybe she won't mind keeping them when you tell her you'll just be at my house for a Bible study."

"Oh, sure. It'll be okay. I just feel a little sorry for her after she's been wrestling Crystal all day to have to get her ready for bed, too."

That night at dinner when Suzanne explained her invitation from Penny, Harriet agreed readily to keep the children for the evening. "We'll have a big time, won't we?" She grinned and poked Randy in the ribs. "You go on, and enjoy yourself. You're too young to do nothing but go to work and come home. You can't enjoy life that way."

Suzanne angled a look at Harriet and wondered what her mother-in-law would say if she knew what an enjoyable time she had had Saturday night with

80

Vincent. Although Harriet seemed completely on Suzanne's side, she had often voiced her hope that Del would change, and that someday they would get back together.

Was Harriet beginning to realize Del would never change? Did her remark just now mean that she would okay a dating relationship for Suzanne with another man? Suzanne doubted it. She dreaded telling her about Vincent, but she knew someday, and soon, she would have to tell her. Although she knew better than to "coach" Randy, she had hoped with all her heart that he wouldn't mention anything to Harriet about Saturday night. Evidently he hadn't, but every time he said, "Grandma, you know what?" her heart would jump.

When dinner was over at last, and Randy still hadn't mentioned anything about Vincent, Suzanne hugged him and suggested, "Why don't you call Jimmy and see if he'd like to come over awhile?" Occupied with a friend, he wouldn't likely give Saturday night another thought, and perhaps he would even forget it all together.

When she called Harriet about four o'clock Tuesday afternoon to remind her she wouldn't be home until nine-thirty or ten, everything still seemed to be all right. "Don't you worry, honey." Harriet's voice was cordial. "The kids will be fine, and so will I. See you later."

Maybe Randy has forgotten it forever, she thought, yet she knew from experience that at the worst possible time Randy would tell Harriet about her date with Vincent. She must talk to Harriet about it. She knew how Del had treated her over the years. Surely she would understand.

She forgot about the children and Harriet, and even Vincent, as she followed Penny's green Volkswagen out of the parking lot and south on Hacienda Boulevard. After a short drive they turned into an apartment house driveway and Penny motioned at the Visitor's Parking area.

"This is it," she called as she got out of her car and locked it. From the parking lot they walked on round concrete steppingstones between two buildings that led to a courtyard and a small square of grass. Several palm trees stretched up to the second story, and red and pink hybiscus bushes bloomed next to a tiny swimming pool. Bird of paradise plants, and other tropicals bordered the walk to the stairway that led to Penny's apartment. Her front door was at the top of the stairs, with barely enough room on the narrow landing to stand comfortably to unlock the door. Her neighbor's entry was about six feet to the left. Penny stepped aside to let Suzanne go in. "Entrez vous."

Her immediate reaction was shock. The living room was so tiny! It probably wasn't as large as her own bedroom. Green shag carpet stretched into the hall and out of sight. The room was dominated by a large, tapistry covered couch. A scarred coffee table in front of it displayed a worn Bible, a three ring binder, and a set of colored pens. A small television set perched on an orange crate in one corner. That was all. What did the sharing group sit on, she wondered. To the right of the front door was a kitchen area with a round table and two chairs. There was an African violet on the table, with more wilted tan leaves than green ones. A Boston fern drooped from a hanger in the corner by the only window. Both rooms seemed to be Comet-clean.

Penny closed the door and whirled around, grinning with pride. "Well? What do you think? Come on, I'll show you the rest." She led the way down a short hall to the bedroom and bath. The bedroom was no larger than the living room but seemed bigger because it contained only a twin bed, a dressing table, and small vanity stool. The bathroom was as tiny as a motor home's. "I just love it." Penny tossed her sweater on the stool and fluffed her hair. "I'm trying to save a little of my salary for furniture. Well, let's get going on the turkey."

They had barely cleared the table when the doorbell sounded. Penny looked up at the ceiling as she rushed to the door. "I don't even have my lipstick on. Hi, John. Come on in." Six feet of smiling, blond energy strode across the room before he saw Suzanne.

"Well, hello. Penny didn't say she had a guest."

"How could I?" She gave him a look that Suzanne couldn't read. "I haven't talked to you since Sunday. Suzanne, this is John Dempsey. He's the teacher."

"I'm not a teacher. I just help the rest of you focus your thoughts. Hi, Suzanne." He nodded and stepped forward as she offered her hand. His handshake was warm and firm. His smile was genuine as he looked directly into her eyes. "Sure glad you could come."

"Suzanne, why don't you sit down?" Penny motioned at the couch. "I'll put on a fresh pot of coffee. You do want some coffee, John?"

"No thanks. Not right now. I'll wait until refreshment time. Are we having refreshments?" Suzanne caught a glint of longing in John's eyes as he watched Penny make coffee. His eyes were light blue, and his thick eyebrows were almost white. Against a deep tan they made him look slightly fierce, but his wide smile and open look denied anything but good humor.

"Refreshments?" Penny looked vague. "Refreshments? Here? Tonight?" Then her eyes crinkled and she smiled. "Yes, John, old Penny's made cookies as usual."

"Chocolate chip?"

"What else?"

He sighed. "That's a relief. You had me worried."

"Knock, knock!" Two women in their early twenties opened the door and came in.

"Just leave the door open," Penny called. "Hi, Pam. Hi, Carole. Introduce them, John."

Before he could begin the introductions, two men and another woman came in. The woman looked to be about Suzanne's age. She stepped to the couch and sat down. "Hello. I'm Dolly, and you are?"

Suzanne smiled. "Suzanne. Penny and I work together."

The two young men sank down on the floor on the television side of the room and leaned against the wall.

"How you doing, Mike? Dave?" John smiled cordially. "Want you all to meet Suzanne, Penny's friend."

Suzanne was impressed with the group. They all had something she couldn't define. Was it a happy glow? They seemed to be full of life, yet calm. She noticed that each person had a Bible and notebook. *They must really take this study seriously*, she thought. Suddenly, she felt out of place. Penny should have told her to bring a Bible. She wasn't sure where it was, but she would have found it.

Penny plugged in the coffee, then grinning, almost skipped to the living room. She picked up her Bible and notebook, sat down on the floor beside Suzanne.

"Here, Penny." Dolly patted the couch.

Penny shook her head. "No—let John sit there. I like the floor." She winked up at Suzanne and slipped a New Testament into her hand.

John sat down on the other side of Dolly and picked up his Bible. "Last week we finished John 13, didn't we?"

Suzanne leaned forward slightly and watched him flip through a few pages. He looked over at her and smiled. Was that a halo around his head, or a ray from the setting sun?

"Okay." His gaze rested a moment on Penny. "As soon as we pray we'll start with John 14." There was a soft flurry of pages as they all opened their Bibles. Suzanne felt blood rush to her cheeks as she fumbled with the New Testament. Where was John 14? She glanced over Penny's shoulder and saw her slowly turning pages: Matthew, Mark, Luke, ah, there it was, John. Not much later than the others she also had her finger in the fourteenth chapter.

"Any prayer requests?" John looked as cheerful as if he were passing around donuts.

Mike held up his hand. "I do." He swallowed. "I'm having a hard time with my temper at work. I pray, and promise the Lord I won't lose my cool, and then I blow it."

John nodded. "Anyone else?"

Carole grinned and bit her lip. Tears glistened in her eyes. "Pray I'll have enough strength to live the way Jesus wants me to around my boyfriend."

Dolly stirred, then took a deep breath. "Well, I don't know what the Bible says about this, but my dog is sick—"

There was subdued tittering in the room.

John lifted his hand and shook his head. "No, no. That's okay, Dolly. The Lord wants us 'in all our ways to consider Him,' that's in Proverbs. What concerns us, concerns Him."

"My dog's at the vet's, and I'm—" She sniffed and drew herself up. "I just don't want him to suffer, that's all."

"Right," John said. "Dave, why don't you start, and I'll close."

Although Suzanne had attended church quite regularly before she and Del were married, she couldn't remember ever going to a prayer meeting, so she was totally unprepared for the prayers she heard:

"Lord, please heal Dolly's dog."

"Help Mike not to get mad at anybody at work, Lord, so he can be a better witness for You."

"Give Carole the strength to resist temptation."

"Jesus," Penny's sweet voice began, "help Suzanne with her problems at home."

Suzanne found herself weeping and was mortified. She fumbled in her purse for a tissue and could only find an old one with chewing gum in one corner, but she managed to pull herself together before the prayers ended. She was awed that people would bare their hearts in public prayer.

During the Bible study, however, she forgot herself and was completely entranced with the words of Jesus. "I am going . . . to prepare a place for you." Heaven must be a wonderful place. But what did He mean when He said, "I am the way and the truth and the life"? And how could He say, "No one comes to the Father except through Me"? She had always heard there were many roads to heaven.

When John closed his Bible he said he would try to answer any questions, but she was too proud and shy to ask. Although she didn't understand or agree with all she had heard, she enjoyed the evening. She felt uplifted, and closer to God than she had since she was a teenager. On the way home she was astonished to realize she hadn't thought of the children, or Vincent, once.

As soon as she walked in, she felt her mother-in-law's iciness. Harriet was watching the ten o'clock news and only flicked an angry glance at Suzanne when she opened the door.

Suzanne smiled. "Hi." She took off her jacket and tossed it on the couch, sat down and pulled off her high heels and wiggled her toes. "How'd it go?"

Harriet's lips were in a tight line. After a long moment she asked, "Suzanne, who is Vincent?"

Suzanne leaned over and picked up a thread off the carpet as she tried to think how to answer Harriet. *I knew I should have told her before Randy did*. But maybe he hadn't said anything about Vincent. In fact, hadn't she introduced him to Randy as "Mr. Marino?" But then, how else could Harriet have known his name? She felt weak, and guilty.

She made herself smile as she looked at Harriet with wide eyes and a puzzled expression. "Vincent?" Her voice sounded unnatural, and she hated herself for being deceitful. Why didn't she tell her? Why this phony act? "Why do you ask?"

"Why?" Harriet's expression was angry. "The man called three times tonight."

Suzanne's heart leaped and she had to bite her lip to keep from smiling. *He called! He still loves me. This, is the time to tell Harriet. Just say it. Just say, Vincent Marino is a man I'm dating.* Instead, she shrugged and shook her head slightly. "There's a client at work named Vincent Marino. He must be trying to reach Mr. Wheatley."

Harriet didn't look convinced. "Strange he'd have your home phone, but not Mr. Wheatley's."

Suzanne couldn't meet Harriet's searching eyes. "He undoubtedly has Mr. Wheatley's number, too." She stood up, stretched, and started toward the hall. She spoke over her shoulder, "How'd you get along with the monsters?"

"Fine. But you shouldn't call them that. They're beautiful, intelligent children." She put her hands on the arms of the chair and pushed herself to a standing position. She groaned and rubbed her knees. "Must be going to rain tonight. My arthritis is killing me." She limped slightly as she crossed the room to turn off the television. "That man wasn't the only one who called."

"Oh?" Suzanne stopped outside Crystal's door and looked back at Harriet. Instead of accusation, there was now a radiant expression on the older woman's face. *Thank heavens she's evidently decided to drop the subject of Vincent.* "Who else called?"

The older woman tried to suppress a smile, then broke into a wide grin. "Del." She walked toward Suzanne.

"What'd he want?" Suzanne's eyes narrowed. "I suppose he can't give us any money this month."

Harriet's grin turned upside down. "Well, I don't know if he'll be able to this month or not. But Suzanne, listen. He called from a drug abuse center."

"Drug abuse?"

Harriet nodded and the grin was back. "He's turned himself in for treatment! Said he hadn't had a drink for a week now." Her eyes glistened, and she reached out and touched Suzanne's shoulder. "Isn't that wonderful?"

CHAPTER 9

SUZANNE FELT AS THOUGH she had struck her head on a cupboard door. She realized her mouth was open and closed it. "Yes." She licked dry lips and tried to smile. "Yes. Wonderful." What did this mean? Was he sincere? Of course. He had to be, or he would never tell Harriet. For two years both women begged him to get help, but he laughed at them. He had scoffed that "cures" were for people who couldn't hold their liquor, and he wasn't about to be sucked into some weak-minded group of alcoholics.

Now he was undergoing treatment himself. *I should be ecstatic, but all I can think of is what will this mean to Vincent and me? Why now, Del? You've messed up my life for years, and now that I*—she took a long, quavering breath and stepped into the nursery.

"Suzanne, are you all right?"

She put a finger to her lips and motioned at the crib. "I'm fine," she whispered. "Tired is all." She covered Crystal, walked quickly down the hall to peek in on Randy, with Harriet limping along behind, then went toward the bathroom. She turned and faced

Harriet. "Think I'll get ready for bed now." Sometimes, if she was putting up her hair, or bathing Crystal, she left the bathroom door open so they could talk, but tonight she closed it firmly. She didn't feel like talking anymore. She had to think.

Frowning, she unbuttoned her blouse and hung it on a hook at the back of the door. She washed and creamed her face, then brushed her teeth. She took off her hose and tossed them in the hamper. How did she feel about Del? She tried to remember what he had been like before he started drinking so much. What sort of man had he been when they married? She closed her eyes for a moment, but couldn't form a mental picture of him when they were newlyweds. She had loved him in the beginning. But she loved Vincent now. Could she love Del again if he stopped drinking?

She stared into her green eyes. *The truth is, I don't want to love Del. Oh, God! I need help.* After ignoring Him all these years, would God help her now?

She opened the door and padded down the hall. "Harriet?"

Harriet was in the kitchen pouring herself a glass of milk. Suzanne smiled apologetically. "I remembered I wanted to check on something tonight. Have you seen my Bible? I can't think what I've done with it."

Harriet took a gulp of milk and nodded. "I think it's on the little shelf by the TV."

Suzanne walked into the living room and picked up the thick little Bible. She looked at it as though seeing it for the first time. Her thumb traced over the index and a bookmark fell out. She leaned over and picked it up. "We read in Saint John tonight."

"Hmmm. That's nice." Harriet took her glass to the sink and ran cold water in it. "Sometimes I read the Psalms when I'm blue."

Suzanne smiled vaguely, then shook her head. She wished she could quit feeling so stunned. But what if

Del wanted to come back? What if he insisted on it? She walked slowly out of the kitchen and down the hall. "Goodnight, Harriet." She turned around. Harriet was following her again. "Thank you for keeping the kids."

"It wasn't any trouble. Del sounded real good, Suzanne."

Suzanne turned the knob on her door. "Did he?" It took all her effort to give her mother-in-law a happy look.

"Sure did. I knew you'd be glad. He said he'd see us soon."

Suzanne nodded, the smile still in place. She edged into her room and almost closed the door. "Harriet? Did Mr. Marino leave any message?"

"No. Said he'd probably call tomorrow."

"Oh. Well, goodnight, then." The latch clicked.

She looked at her white face in the mirror and whispered, "I don't want to see you, Del." She turned to get a side view of herself. She was almost as slender as Penny. Her copper-colored hair looked good, too. The new style was curly and feminine around her face and at the neck. It was easy to keep and made her feel professional and chic. Del was in the process of changing, but she had already changed.

She opened a drawer and took out a new waltz length blue nightie. She had bought it on impulse one day last week on her lunch hour. Why had she bought it? No one would see it under her bathrobe. She held it up, and swaying back and forth, she whispered, "I bought it for you, darling, my darling Vincent." She was appalled at her thoughts, and felt herself blush. But wasn't she justified to dream? He'd told her over and over he wanted to marry her. She would have to give him her answer next Sunday. Her heart's answer was yes, but what about Del? She put the lovely gown back in the drawer and put on old pajamas.

She turned on the bed lamp, threw back the spread,

and got in bed. She adjusted the pillow against the headboard and leafed through the Bible until she came to the New Testament. *Now, Saint John, I know you're here some place. Matthew, Mark . . .* In the book of Mark the subtitle "Divorce" leaped out at her and she drew in her breath. "I knew it was in the Bible someplace," she mumbled. As she read the passage her heart pounded. When she had read it all, she put the Bible down and closed her eyes. A tear slid down her cheek.

The next morning, each time the office phone rang Suzanne jumped. At eleven-thirty her spirits sank. Vincent wasn't going to call. It had been a trying morning. She hadn't slept well last night. Every bitter memory of Del kept fighting with every sweet thought of Vincent, and the word "adultery" was always before her. She probably hadn't gotten over two hours sleep, and felt exhausted. She even had a headache. Penny, of course, was her usual exuberant self, and wanted to talk about the Bible study. Suzanne didn't feel like discussing it. She couldn't share Penny's enthusiasm because she wished she hadn't gone. If she hadn't gone she wouldn't have opened her own Bible at home, and wouldn't have read for herself what Jesus said about divorce and remarriage.

Suddenly the reception door swept open, and Vincent stood there, out of breath and smiling. In a white tee shirt and faded jeans he seemed to Suzanne the most handsome man in the world.

"I made it!" His smile dazzled her. "I was sure you'd be gone for lunch." He crossed the room, his heavy safety shoes leaving faint dusty prints on the carpet. "Hi, Penny." He gave her a wink, then looked at Suzanne. "Hello, Miss Hard-to-get-a-hold-of." His eyes were soft. "Please forgive my work clothes. But I had to see you."

Suzanne walked to the low partition. "I'm glad

you're here." In spite of Penny's alert interest, she carefully studied his face, his brows, his lips. She thrilled at the open love in his eyes. "You look great." Her voice caressed him.

He glanced at Penny and cleared his throat. "How does McDonald's sound to you? I can't go anywhere fancy, looking like this."

Suzanne blinked, as though waking from a dream. "Why don't you come home with me?" She was shocked at her question. How could she take Vincent home with Harriet there? On the other hand, why shouldn't she? It was her home! She could bring anyone she wanted. So what if Harriet was counting on her and Del getting back together? And if Del was trying to straighten up, that was his problem. She had worried about him long enough. As for adultery? Who knows what the Bible really means anyhow?

"You mean your house for lunch?"

"Of course. Let me call my mother-in-law, so she can put another wiener in the pan!"

Vincent laughed, then looked at his watch. "That would be great, some other time. But I really think I'd better grab a quick sandwich. I've got a crane coming at one-thirty, and I don't want to pay for standby time."

Suzanne let out her breath. "Okay. McDonald's it is." She smiled up at him and reached for the phone. "I still have to call Harriet and tell her I won't be there." She pushed the buttons and waited. After a moment she put the receiver down. "Busy."

Penny waved at them. "Why don't you two go on and I'll call your house for you?"

"Would you?" Suzanne got her purse and was out the gate before Penny could answer. "Just tell her I couldn't get home today, but I'll see her tonight."

In a blue and white pickup truck, Suzanne sat close to Vincent during the short distance to the drive-in. It was all she could do to keep from throwing her arms around him. During a too short lunch their hands touched and their eyes spoke love. Suzanne started to tell him about Del, but decided their time together was too short to ruin it. Maybe she would tell him Sunday.

In the office parking lot Vincent let his arms rest across the back of the seat. He looked down at her. "I'll come for you about nine-thirty Sunday morning. Is that too early?"

"I can drive."

"No, no. I want to be sure you get there."

She put her hands on her hips. "Thanks a lot. You said I was a good driver."

"You are. But that station wagon of yours needs some work."

"Oh. Okay, master. We'll be ready at nine-thirty."

Heedless of people leaving or returning for lunch, he took her in his arms. She pressed into his chest, welcoming the touch of his body. After a long kiss, he pushed back slightly, and she moved away. Neither could speak for a moment. He cleared his throat. "I don't want to, Suzanne, but I have to leave."

She pushed down on the door handle. "I know." He started to open his door. "No, don't get out. It's okay." She jumped out, ran around to the front of the truck and looked up at him. "I'll see you Sunday." She waved and ran to the building. When she turned again he was already out of the driveway.

The rest of the day was a blur to Suzanne. She wasn't sure what she did. It was all mechanical. The only thing she was sure of was that she was in love.

At home that night, Harriet's mood had turned icy again. Suzanne made several attempts to get the conversation rolling, but at best she only got a grunt or two from the older woman. While making salad, Suzanne finally blurted,

"Harriet, what's wrong with you?"

"What's wrong with me?" She banged a spoon against a pan and her brown eyes flashed. "What's wrong with *you*?" She stamped across the floor and threw the spoon into the sink. "So you had lunch with your lover, Vincent. Your boss's client, my foot! You with two babies at home and a sick husband."

Suzanne caught her breath. "How dare you speak to me like that." Her voice was a grating whisper. She hoped Randy wouldn't hear from the living room.

"Well, it's true." Harriet made no effort to keep her voice down. "That nice little girl in your office told me all about it."

Suzanne closed her eyes for a moment. *Thanks, Penny.* Yet it wasn't Penny's fault. She wasn't a gossip, and it wouldn't occur to her to be deceitful. Vincent had taken Suzanne to lunch. Penny would see nothing wrong in that, so why should she cover up?

"Of course I had lunch with Mr. Marino. So what? Can't I have a male friend? You'd think nothing of it if I had lunch with Penny, or Selena." She glared at Harriet. "What's wrong with having lunch with *any* friend?" Her heart beat faster and her breathing was shallow.

"I knew last night you didn't love my son. And me doing everything I can to help save his marriage."

"Del has nothing to do with this."

"How long have you been sneaking around behind my back?"

"Harriet! I won't stand for you to talk to me like that."

"Then maybe you'd just better get yourself another slave."

"Fine. You can leave any time." Her hands trembled as she put the salad in the refrigerator and dug in her purse for the car keys. "I'll drive you."

Harriet was already putting on a sweater. "No, thank you." She rushed down the hall to the front door and swung it open. She gave Suzanne one last withering look, stepped outside and banged the door shut. Appalled, Suzanne watched her mother-in-law scurry down the walk.

Suzanne bit on her fist to keep from crying. "Oh, no," she moaned. "What have I done?"

"What happened, Mommy?" Randy stood at her elbow, his eyes fearful.

Suzanne dropped to her knees and pressed his trembling body to hers. "Oh, Randy. I hurt Grandma's feelings. She's not going to baby-sit you kids anymore."

"Can't you tell her you're sorry?"

Suzanne shook her head. "It's too late. She's really angry." Tears spilled out and she wiped them away with her fingers.

"Don't cry, Mommy." His own voice was tearful. "Cheryl can baby-sit us."

"No!" Suzanne's voice was too loud. She swallowed and tried to calm herself. She forced herself to smile at Randy. "No, Cheryl can't come because she's in college during the day." She took a deep breath. "I'll think of something. Come on, let's get Crystal and eat our dinner."

When dinner was over and both children in bed, she called Justin. It was the first time she had ever had to call him at home. He answered on the first ring.

"Justin, I hate to bother you, but I've got a problem. My mother-in-law, can't—she can't keep the children tomorrow."

"You mean you can't come in?"

"I'm wracking my brain for a sitter, but right now, zero."

"Well. . . ." There was a soundless space between them.

"I'll keep trying to think of something, Justin, someone."

"Hey, don't sweat it. I'll be in court in the morning anyway. Penny'll be there. We'll work it out."

"Thank you, Justin. I'll be in if I possibly can."

She called Selena then, and although her neighbor asked questions, Suzanne didn't tell her about the quarrel with Harriet, but only that she needed a baby-sitter for "a day or two."

"Well, keedo, I would be glad to help you out, but I have to circulate a petition tomorrow."

"No, I wasn't asking you, Selena. I know you're busy. I thought maybe Cheryl had some girl friend who could work during the day."

"I'll try to find out, and let you know, okay?"

She called Penny and told her she wouldn't be there in the morning, at least for awhile. "You don't know anyone at church who would sit, do you?"

Penny said she'd ask around. "And I'll pray, too, Suzanne."

Although exhausted, Suzanne couldn't go to sleep. She kept hearing Harriet's ugly words of accusation. Yes, the truth hurt. It was true she didn't love her son, Del, and she did love Vincent. She didn't blame Harriet for being angry and disappointed. No wonder she left. And what was Suzanne going to do if she couldn't find someone to stay with the children? She couldn't quit her job. She needed the income too badly.

In the darkness of her room she spoke softly. "God? If You hear me, would You please help me? I don't know what I'm going to do about work. You know I've got to have somebody reliable to take care of Randy and Crystal. If You have time, would You mind trying to find someone?" Tears streamed from her eyes and dampened her hair and her pillow. At last sleep took over.

Suzanne woke before the alarm the next morning. *How ironic*, she thought. *How I'd love to sleep in on work days, and now that I can, I can't!* She put on her bathrobe and went to the kitchen to make coffee. She heard a soft knock at the front door and tiptoed to the window to peek out. Harriet was standing there. Suzanne opened the door and Harriet smiled meekly.

"May I come in?"

"Of course." She allowed Harriet plenty of room.

"I decided it wasn't a very Christian thing to do, leaving you without anybody to take care of the children."

"We'll manage."

Harriet inched past Suzanne and moved slowly toward the kitchen. Frowning, Suzanne followed. Harriet took off her sweater, draped it over the back of a chair, and put her purse on top of the refrigerator.

"I want to apologize for accusing you. I'm sorry. It's like you said, why shouldn't you have men friends? I've known you for twelve years, Suzanne, and I've never known you to be anything but true-blue to Del. So I should've realized you are still the same, still wanting the best for Del and the children."

"But Harriet, I've changed."

"I know. You're much thinner and even prettier. I can't wait for Del to see you now."

Suzanne let out her breath in a rush. *Why am I such a chicken! Why don't I tell this woman I'm madly in love with another man, and I don't ever want to see her son again?*

"So, honey, I hope you can forgive and forget what I said last night. I'm truly sorry. Now, you'd better shake a leg, and get ready for work."

Suzanne fled to the bathroom, hating herself for backing down, yet thankful Harriet had returned. Thankful? Had God caused this? Maybe God had heard her and helped Harriet change her mind. She experienced a fleeting sense of awe. But would it last? What about Sunday? It would be just a matter of time until Harriet found out. *I'll tell her about Vincent this morning before I go to work.* But even as she put on her makeup, she knew she wouldn't tell her about him, at least until she gave him an answer to his marriage proposal.

Sunday was a typical Los Angeles gray and gloomy morning until a weak sun began to warm the basin. Vincent had picked them up right on time, and the Cadillac had just rounded a curve and topped a hill on Highway 39 when Randy said, "I didn't know you lived on a mountain. Do you have a horse?"

Vincent laughed. "No, but my daughter Carla used to have a horse. I might get another one for Kristen."

"Who's Kristen?"

Suzanne looked at Vincent apologetically. "I told you, Randy. Kristen is his granddaughter."

"Is she a baby?"

"Not exactly." Vincent glanced up at Randy in the rear view mirror. "She's three, going on twelve."

Randy jerked his head and frowned. "What?"

"I'm kidding. But she's very grown up for her age."

The car made an abrupt turn off the two-lane highway and moved slowly up a long, tree-lined driveway. An enormous Spanish style house, white stucco with red tiled roof, dominated the hilltop. On the drive up Suzanne got glimpses of fiery bougainvillaea, hillsides aglow with pink, red, and blue flowers, and endless lawns. When they stopped in front of wide steps and an arched portico, the front door opened and a little girl with brooding eyes and pouty lips stepped out.

Vincent opened the car door. "There's my Kristen," he called to her. The girl didn't answer, but took a few steps toward him. He leaned down, looked in the car and winked at Suzanne. "In her usual good humor, I see." He moved around the car quickly and opened the doors. Before Suzanne could get out, he had unbuckled Crystal's safety seat and picked her up. Kristen stood beside her grandfather, holding up her arms.

"Granddad can't take you right this minute, Kristen, okay?"

"No!" She began to cry and hug his leg.

Randy got out of the car and stood stiffly beside Suzanne. He shook his head with disgust. "What a crybaby," he mumbled.

Vincent rolled his eyes at Suzanne. "Well, it's a start."

Inside the house Suzanne stopped, wide-eyed, spellbound.

"Well, my darling Suzanne, what do you think?"

She was speechless. Wherever she looked there was opulent beauty. She had never been in a home like this. There were velvet chairs and couches; the dark red carpet seemed like a foam rubber mattress underfoot; there were crystal chandeliers, and a grand piano. Statues and plants graced the old-style salon, cut glass bowls and vases were on every table.

Numbly, she took Crystal out of his arms and held her tightly.

"What's wrong? Was I holding her wrong?"

"No. Nothing like that. It's just that if she gets loose, she could make a shambles of this in two minutes."

He threw back his head and laughed.

"Seriously, I don't think we belong here," Suzanne said in a small voice. "I didn't know you were this rich."

He put his arms around her waist and squeezed her. "I told you I can take care of you."

"Hold me now, Granddad." Kristen's arms were up, and her face was a tiny storm cloud.

"Okay, okay, little Miss Jealousy." Vincent swooped her up in his arms. "Where's Mommy?"

"By the fimming poo."

"We'll go see her."

Kristen's frown was fierce as she pointed a thin finger at Suzanne. "Mommy said she's not going to be nice to her!"

CHAPTER 10

THE PREMONITION SUZANNE FELT on board the Queen Mary had come true. It was going to be hopeless; Carla Marino had already made up her mind against her and had already influenced the child.

Kristen, now smugly secure in her grandfather's arms, glared down at Suzanne over his shoulder. Her face rested in the curve of his neck and her arms hugged him possessively. Suzanne looked up at her, and forced herself to smile, but Kristen stuck out her tongue, then turned away. Suzanne's mouth opened, then she bit her lip. She couldn't remember any child disliking her. All of Randy's friends seemed to love her. There was an actual pain in the area of her heart, and tears formed beneath her eyelids. Frantic thoughts whipped around in her mind. She wanted to grab her son and run away from Vincent's hostile daughter and spoiled grandchild, but she couldn't do that. Even if Vincent let her go, she couldn't walk home, especially carrying Crystal part of the time. She hoisted the heavy baby to the other arm. If only she had insisted on driving her car.

She tried to see Vincent's face, but he had walked a few steps ahead of her into the great living room. What was he thinking? He hadn't reprimanded Kristen for the unkind remark. He hadn't said a word.

He stopped suddenly and put her down. "Whew! You're getting heavy. Why don't you see if you can race Randy to the big tree by the pool?" Kristen frowned up at him, then stared at Randy, her brown eyes defiant, lower lip out, and a challenge in her jaw line.

Randy stared back. "I can beat a girl any time."

"Ho, ho! We'll see. She's a pretty fast runner." Vincent pointed to the double glass doors across the room. "Let's go out on the patio to start this great race."

Randy ran to the other side, with Kristen right beside him. As Suzanne crossed the luxurious room she held Crystal with a viselike grip. The baby's blond head seemed to be on a swivel, always watching for an opportunity to grab something.

"Why don't you put her down?" Vincent asked. "She's too heavy for you."

Suzanne shook her head. "Nothing would be safe."

Out on the patio Suzanne was again astonished at the beauty of her surroundings. The patio itself was huge. Bigger than her own living room at home, she estimated it to be around thirty feet wide. The floor was a beautiful pattern of sandstone and brick.

Everywhere she looked there were flowers blooming. There were several azaleas in large wooden tubs, laden with pink, lavender, and white blossoms. Ivy geraniums in ceramic containers contributed their color, along with other flowers Suzanne didn't recognize. Chaise lounges and chairs, each with a table placed conveniently next to it, were arranged for comfort and the view, which was breathtaking. A great expanse of lawn carpeted the gentle slope down to a sparkling oval pool. A curving flagstone path, bordered on each side with sweet alyssum, led from the house down to a cabana.

A perfectly formed young woman in a white bikini was sunbathing on the deck. Carla. Her mouth tightened. She dreaded the moment when Vincent would introduce them. Yet, in spite of the shock and sadness Carla's apparent attitude had caused, she couldn't help thinking that if she married Vincent, she would live in this Eden.

"Mom," Randy pulled her hand, "can we go swimming?"

Suzanne shrugged, afraid to trust her voice.

"We'll go swimming later." Vincent put his hand on Randy's shoulder. "Right now we're going to have a race. Now, Randy, you're bigger and faster than Kristen. How about if you let her start first. Do you think you can still beat her?"

Randy screwed up his face, then brightened. "I sure can."

Vincent smiled. "We'll let her get to that little tree, then you can go. Will that be okay?"

"Okay." Randy was already in running position.

"And one other thing," Vincent said. He looked first at Kristen's upturned face, then Randy's. "Never, never run on the deck around the pool."

"Why?" Randy asked.

"Oh, Randy," Suzanne half-scolded. "You know why. You learned that in your first swimming lesson."

"Tell him, Kristen. Why don't we run on the deck?"

For the first time Suzanne saw beauty in the little girl's face. Her eyes opened wide and her mouth lost its petulant droop. "'Cause we fip and fall down."

"Right. We slip and fall. Now ready?"

As soon as the children were racing down the hill, Vincent turned to Suzanne with anxiety in his eyes. "Suzanne, I know your feelings are hurt. Here, let me hold Crystal." He took the baby and absently pressed his lips to her fat cheek. "And I know that Kristen acts like a spoiled brat. Please don't let what she said upset you. Anyway, Carla probably didn't say it. Kristen's been known to lie. And if she did say it, so what?" He put his free arm around Suzanne and drew her as close as she would let him. "Listen, nothing is going to come between us."

There was a jarring crash of metal and glass. Suzanne looked in time to see Carla leap up from her chair, screaming and wiping at herself with a towel. Suzanne couldn't hear the words, but the tone was angry, and it was directed at her son.

"What in the world?" Vincent thrust Crystal in her arms and loped down the path, with Suzanne following. Randy began to run toward them at the same time. Suzanne could see, even at that distance, that he was frightened.

"What's wrong, Randy?" she heard Vincent ask, but Randy raced past him, openly bawling by this time, and in moments was hanging on to Suzanne.

"What's wrong?" Suzanne sat Crystal on the grass and stooped to face him. "Randy! Hush. What happened?"

"There was a TV tray," Randy wailed, "and I stubbed my toe on it, and all the ice and drink spilled all over that lady."

Suzanne saw Carla grab Kristen's hand and they both hurried up the hill, away from Suzanne, toward the back of the house.

Vincent knelt beside Randy, "Are you hurt?"

"He's not hurt." Suzanne's voice was strained. "He's scared, and embarrassed."

Vincent stood up, smiling. "Well, then. If you're not hurt, let's get on with this day." He swooped Randy up on his shoulders. Randy didn't smile. He looked miserable and his lower lip trembled. Vincent looked up at him. "Come on, cheer up. I know your mom brought your swim trunks."

"I don't want to go swimming." Randy's voice was almost inaudible. "I want to go home."

Suzanne looked down at the spot where she had placed Crystal and gasped. "Where's Crystal?" Her voice rose. "Vincent? Where is she?" She cupped her hand to her mouth and screamed, "Crystal!"

Vincent put Randy down and looked around. "Now, don't get excited. She can't be far." He looked toward the pool, uttered a strange sound and began to run. Suzanne stared at the scene. Crystal was by the side of the pool. Horrified, she watched the baby take a few faltering steps and topple into the water. Screaming, she began to run the short distance, but the baby was already in the water. Vincent would never reach her in time. Her own legs felt out of control and she fell headlong in the grass.

Whimpering, almost crazy with fear, she leaped up and saw Vincent dive into the water. In one fluid motion he got an arm under Crystal and lifted the soggy little form out of the water. In seconds he placed her on the deck and hoisted himself beside her. When Suzanne reached the pool Crystal was gasping and crying, sputtering and coughing. Vincent had her over his shoulder, patting her and crooning soft words. Too weak to stand, she sank down on the hot cement beside them. It was unbelievable. She closed her eyes in thanksgiving. *She's alive.*

"She's okay!" Vincent breathed. He held her out so they could look at her. "Good color. I don't think we need the paramedics."

Unnoticed, Randy stood looking down at them, white as a statue, until a completely recovered Crystal began to howl out her indignation. Then he yelled, "Whew! I'm glad she's not drownded."

With a little cry, Suzanne jumped up, took the baby away from Vincent, and began half-walking, half-running up the hill. *My baby almost drowned!* She should never have come to this place. As soon as she

105

could trust her voice, she would ask Vincent to take them home. She wasn't wanted here, anyway. In the awful time just past, she had almost forgotten that Carla swore at Randy, and now she also remembered how Carla went into the house without ever acknowledging her presence. Oh, yes, she had to get away from this place. She felt Vincent's arm around her waist and stiffened. His arm felt cold and his clothes were still wet. He had taken off his shoes and socks, but he still towered over her. She pulled away.

"What's wrong?"

She kept walking. Although she loved him, she could never be happy in this situation. She glanced at him. "Would you please take us home?"

His mouth opened slightly and his brows came down. "Now? What do you mean? You haven't been here an hour."

"And look what's happened!" She began to cry and her voice rose. "My baby almost drowned, and your daughter swore at my son. She hates us."

"I'm sorry for the way she acts, Suzanne. But I don't know how to make her change. She's full of such anger, such bitterness. Suzanne, her mother and I would not approve the idea of her marriage at such an early age. But she went against our wishes and married anyway. Now she is only nineteen, divorced, and has a small child. I guess I haven't always known how to manage, but she isn't really a terrible person. She used to be so like her mother." He looked at her closely, and his voice softened. "Please. I want you to spend the day here. Nell made us a good lunch. Randy can go swimming. We can all go swimming. We can lie in the sun." He looked as though he was near crying himself. "I need you with me."

Suzanne wavered. She drew in a shuddering breath, and wiped tears from her eyes. She loved to swim and sunbathe. But more than anything, she loved Vincent. "I'm so sorry. Somehow, we've gotten off to a bad start. I think it'd be better if the kids and I go home now."

He sighed and turned up his palms. "All right. If that's what you want." He looked away, out beyond the swimming pool. There was a pained expression on his face and he looked older to Suzanne. In the bright sunlight she could see many fine lines she had never noticed before. But somehow, he seemed even dearer. "Oh, Vincent! It isn't really what I want." Crystal squirmed and fretted in her arms. She finally let the wet, wiggling baby slip down on the grass, but she held her hand firmly. "I guess I really want to be with you."

"Then don't go! Randy, you want to stay, don't you?"

"Not 'specially."

"I thought you wanted to go swimming?"

"I did, but. . . ." His eyes slid away from Vincent and back to the pool.

"Well! Let's get our suits on."

Vincent began to grin, and the sparkle came back to his eyes. "We don't want the kids to be afraid of the water." Impulsively, he hugged her and gave her a robust kiss on the mouth. Randy's mouth opened in surprise, and Suzanne saw Carla looking down at them from an upstairs window. When he released her Crystal was trotting toward the pool.

Suzanne ran after her and was laughing by the time she grabbed her. "I don't think we have to worry about this one having any fear of water."

Randy took a cue from his mother's laughter. "Me, neither." He put his hands together. "I'm going to learn to dive like you."

Vincent laughed, relief and joy on his face. "Come on, I'll show you where to change."

He led them through a French door to a sun room, filled with almost every kind of house plant, and into a small bedroom. "The bathroom is just to the left there. I'll put my suit on and meet you at the pool."

In a few minutes the three of them were dressed, picked up their towels, and went out to the patio. He was already there, tanned and magnificent in white trunks. Suzanne suddenly felt shy and self-conscious, and pulled the cover-up around her tightly. Vincent didn't seem to notice her, however, and challenged Randy.

In the water Vincent took full charge of Crystal and Randy, allowing Suzanne the freedom of swimming and diving without having to worry. Randy was a good swimmer for his age, and the air echoed with his shouts of pleasure. Crystal apparently had forgotten her frightening episode and seemed to love the water. Vincent coached Randy on diving, and encouraged the baby to put her head under and blow bubbles. After a few minutes, Suzanne got out and spread her towel on one of the chaise lounges. The sun felt wonderful, and for the moment she was in a dream world. She was surrounded by luxury, and the man she loved seemed to love her children.

She was almost asleep when Vincent deposited a wet and cold baby on her stomach. "I think she's a little chilled. Anyway, I'm hungry. Let's go inside and see what Nell fixed for us."

They took the lunch of cold fried chicken, potato salad, a fresh fruit salad, chocolate cake, and milk into the sun room. The food was delicious, seasoned with conversation and bursts of laughter. Suzanne marveled at how comfortable she felt with him.

Halfway through lunch Crystal began to rub her eyes and yawn. Her blue eyes were almost closed when Vincent lifted her out of the chair and put her on the soft carpet. She started to struggle, but sighed deeply and gave into sleep, her arms and legs flopped out toward the four corners of the room.

After lunch Randy began to walk around the room, looking bored. "Do you have anything for kids to do?"

"Sure." Vincent stood up, pushing him gently toward a built-in set of drawers. "Look in those last two." Surprised and smiling, Randy took out a set of Legos and began to build.

Vincent sat down beside Suzanne and took her hand. He looked so deep into her eyes she felt fire in the pit of her stomach. "My sweet, sweet Suzanne. Are you ready to give me your answer?"

She leaned toward him slightly and studied his face. She touched his lips with her fingers, tracing the shape of his mouth. How she loved him! He was handsome, powerful, kind, romantic. He stirred her more than Del ever had. Yes, yes, her heart cried. Marry him! As she opened her lips to speak, a slight movement on the other side of the room caught her attention. She turned to look at the door. There, her face ugly with anger, stood Carla.

CHAPTER 11

HOW LONG HAD CARLA been watching them? Suzanne noticed things about her appearance she hadn't seen at a distance. Her long hair was permed and bleached, bushing about her face and shoulders like a parka. Alluring curls floated over her forehead and in front of her ears. Her dark eyebrows were arched, and her lips were full. Beautiful. Wild, but beautiful.

When Suzanne's eyes had widened at sight of Carla, Vincent turned. His soft, loving expression of a moment before turned to anger. He leaped up, bumping the table. "Carla. What are you doing here?"

Carla had fury in her eyes. "What am I doing here?" She stepped into the room, and stood with one hand on her hip. Her designer jeans revealed every curve of her legs and hips. Her white, scoop-necked blouse was cut low. "I live here, remember?"

"Don't be impudent, Carla."

She glared at her father, then waved a hair dryer at him, and in a metallic whisper, grated, "I came to get this." Vincent's eyes narrowed and an eyebrow lifted. "If you don't believe me, then don't!"

His shoulders sagged. "Okay, okay. Come on in and I'll introduce you to Mrs. Forrest." Uncomfortable and embarrassed, Suzanne had been staring at the floor, but when Vincent put his hand on her shoulder, she looked up at him. "As you already know, this is my daughter, Carla."

Suzanne's green eyes were calm as she turned toward the younger woman, and she managed a smile. "Hello, Carla."

Carla's eyes were brown, but they lacked Vincent's warmth and intense color. She stared at Suzanne, unsmiling.

She really hates me, Suzanne thought. Yet, if Vincent and I are ever to be happy, I'll have to win her friendship. She glanced at Randy, who had made himself as small as possible beside an open drawer. "I'm sorry my son overturned your drink."

Carla shrugged and her mouth turned down. She dismissed Suzanne with a slow blink and turned her eyes on Vincent. "Can I have the keys to the Porsche?"

"The Porsche? What's wrong with your Camaro?"

"Dead battery."

"Carla." He shook his head. "Why would you let that happen?"

"It's not my fault."

"Of course not. You didn't have any warning, no sluggish starts—"

"I turned the key and it was dead, that's all!" Her hard eyes pinned him.

The muscles in his jaws tightened. "Where do you have to go?"

"Oh, please." Her eyes rolled up. "Forget it. I'll get a ride." She whirled around, then looked back with a toss of her head. "My thumb's still good."

As she disappeared into Nell's room he thundered, "The keys are on the bureau." He drew a breath between clenched teeth. "And call the auto club."

111

The hall door slammed and a wild-eyed Crystal sat up, screaming.

"Oh for. . . ." Vincent groaned and raised his hands, as Suzanne rushed to pick up the baby. "I'm sorry, Suzanne. That daughter of mine."

"Shh," she murmured, both to Crystal and to him. "It's okay, it's okay."

"It's not okay." He walked slowly to the window, beating a fist into his hand. He folded his arms across his chest, and stared out at the empty pool. "She's beyond me. I don't know how to handle her." In a voice Suzanne could barely hear he added, "I can't believe she'd be that rude to you."

Suzanne wiped the tears from Crystal's face and neck. It always amazed her how a baby could manufacture so much salt water in a few seconds. Standing, rocking back and forth, she patted Crystal until she quit crying. "Vincent." Her eyes glowed up at him. "Please don't worry about me. It'll be all right. In time. Somehow I'll make friends with her."

He turned to face her, his frown gradually relaxing. The soft look came back in his eyes and he whispered, "Is that a yes to my question?"

Suzanne turned to look at Randy who was pretending indifference as he played, but she knew he was listening. She turned back to Vincent and bit her lip. "I've got something to tell you," she murmured, "about Del."

"Del?" He frowned. "What about him?"

"Harriet said he called—the same night you did. He's in some rehabilitation place, to quit drinking."

Vincent searched her eyes. "Well, that's good, isn't it?"

"Yes, of course. Except. . . ." She looked away. "If he's cured, if there's no reason. . . ." She glanced at Randy again.

"Oh." Vincent nodded. After a moment he pursed his lips. "Are you telling me you would be reconciled?"

She closed her eyes, hugged the baby, and rocked back and forth. "I don't know. I don't know."

Randy came to Suzanne and looked up at her, frowning.

"What's reconcile mean?" A trace of fear was in his eyes.

"Nothing that concerns you, darling." She hugged him. "I think you'd better put away your toys now." She smiled at Vincent. "And, we'd better go. Thank you for a lovely time." At his derisive look she continued, "No, no. I mean it. It's been . . ." She compressed her lips as her mind replayed the tension-filled day. Her mouth trembled on a smile. "It's always wonderful to be with you." She moved closer to him, and his gentle bear hug included all three of them.

That evening, after the children were in bed, Suzanne decided to go through her clothes. It was almost summer, and some of her clothes were too warm in the office, even with air conditioning. As she took summer things out of the closet, she was glad she hadn't thrown them away when she gained weight. She tried on a white dress that was at least six years old, and it fit her perfectly. She tried on a light blue skirt and a couple of summer blouses. With a button here, and a seam there, she would have three different outfits.

It was almost midnight when she finished washing and pressing the clothes. She looked in on the children, still in the druglike sleep fresh air and exercise produce. But even though she had been outside and exercising too, she knew she would never sleep the way her thoughts were whipping around. She kept seeing Crystal topple into the pool. When she rejected that horrible memory, angry recollections of Carla took over. Pushing those thoughts out, Del and Vincent took her mind: then the cycle would begin again. After a long hot shower, and positive her mind would never quit whirling, she got in bed. *At least I have something different to wear tomorrow,* she thought, and fell asleep before she could pull the sheet up over her shoulders.

"You look pretty and summery in that white dress," Penny smiled at Suzanne.

"You look like a summer sky, yourself," Suzanne grinned. "You look good in blue."

"You got some tan over the weekend, didn't you?"

Suzanne felt herself blushing. Although Penny knew Vincent had taken her to lunch, Suzanne had never told her how much she cared for him. She didn't know whether to tell her about yesterday or not. Then she thought of Crystal's near disaster, and knew she wouldn't be able to keep that a secret.

Without revealing her feelings about Vincent, she stated facts. Mr. Marino had a granddaughter Randy's age, and he invited them to go swimming. Penny was horrified when she heard that Crystal almost drowned. "And yet," she said, "there's a lot to thank the Lord for."

Suzanne gaped. As she worked at her desk that morning she tried to think of a way she could show God she was thankful for sparing Crystal's life, but she could think of nothing magnificent enough.

About eleven o'clock the reception door opened. Suzanne's eyes widened and she drew in a quick breath. Carla, dressed more flamboyantly than yesterday, stepped in and closed the door. She had on a sheer lavender dress, with a plaid design woven in satin. There was a delicate ruffle and bow at the neck. Although the sleeves were long and cuffed with ruffles, they were sheer enough to reveal her bronze arms. She wore lavender hose, and a slightly darker shade of lavender high heels. A small purse, the same shade as her shoes, dangled from her shoulder. She could have been a model for Vogue.

"Good morning," Penny flashed her beautiful smile. "May I help you?"

Suzanne stood up quickly and walked toward the divider. *What is she doing here? Is something wrong with Vincent?* "Hello, Carla. Is anything wrong?" She crossed the room.

Arrogantly, with her eyes half closed, Carla smiled. "Not yet. But I would like to talk to you."

Suzanne frowned as she looked at her watch. *What on earth would she want to talk about?* She could feel Penny's curious gaze. She licked her lips. "I go to lunch in about fifteen minutes. Can we talk then?"

Carla glanced at Penny, shrugged and made the same ugly, mouth-turned-down expression Suzanne had seen yesterday. The awful grimace seemed incongruous on such a beautiful face. Her lips tightened as her cool eyes focused on Suzanne. "There's a new pizza place half a block from here."

"Susie," Justin Wheatley bellowed as he charged out of the hallway. He stopped short when he saw Carla. "Oh." He ogled her, taking her in from blond hair to lavender shoes. He seemed momentarily stunned. Under his admiring scrutiny she became a different person: soft, enchanting. Her eyes danced up at him, and she tilted her head in an adorable, childlike way. The complete change astounded Suzanne. For a full moment she stared at Carla. At last she spoke. "Justin, this is Vincent Marino's daughter, Carla." She turned to Carla who hadn't taken her eyes off Justin. "Miss Marino, this is my boss, Justin Wheatley, and," she motioned toward the desk, "our receptionist, Penny Davidson."

Penny said, "How do you do?" but neither Justin nor Carla paid any attention. He took her hand, and covered it with the other. "Carla," Justin exuded charm. "A name with mysterious promise."

What a ham, Suzanne thought. It hadn't been many weeks ago that he had been making over her.

"What can Justin David Wheatley, Counselor, do for such a lovely one as you?"

"What would the Counselor like to do for me?" Her eyes were Fourth of July sparklers. Then she laughed and gently took her hand from his. "Actually, Mr. Wheatley—"

"Please. Your father calls me Justin."

Her laugh was bell-like. "Justin. That's an odd name. Oops!" She tittered again. "I mean, not odd." She leaned toward him and he touched her arm, smiling down into her eyes. "But anyhow, Justin, I came to see your secretary on a personal matter."

Justin's eyebrows raised as he glanced at Suzanne. "Oh? Well, okay." He faced her, and his green eyes burned. "But when are you going to see me on a personal matter?"

Penny and Suzanne looked at each other, then up at the ceiling.

"Well, my telephone number is the same as my dad's."

Justin beamed his pleasure. He went back toward his office, turned and waved. When his door closed Suzanne said, "It's almost time for my lunch hour. I'll go wash up and be right with you."

Suzanne washed and dried her hands, put on lipstick, and combed her hair. With her hand on the door she glanced at the full length mirror. "Oh, phooey," she whispered. "My hem is coming out." She found the tiny mending packet, threaded a needle, and whipped off her skirt. She was taking long stitches when Penny rushed in.

"Miss Marino wants to know how much longer you'll be?"

Suzanne's eyes widened. "I couldn't have been in here over three minutes! Tell her about my skirt, and suggest she go get us a booth."

When Suzanne entered the Italian restaurant, the spicy smell made her ravenous. Yet, seeing Carla lounging at a table and staring at her like a vixen, took away her appetite.

"I ordered a pepperoni for us to share," Carla said.

"Thank you." Suzanne looked around. It was a typical pizza restaurant. Italian prints, lots of plants, and a wall of video games.

A teenage boy in a large chef's hat brought a tray to their table. Carla looked at him and smiled. "Pepperoni is my favorite—almost." She simpered at him, and he grinned in a worshipful way, stumbled slightly over a corner of the bench.

Suzanne stared at the woman across the table. How could anyone as wonderful as Vincent sire anyone as shallow and hateful? "Carla," impatience was barely covered in her voice, "what did you want to see me about?"

Carla slowly opened her mouth, staring at Suzanne all the while, and put the pointed end of a steaming piece of pizza in her mouth, bit it and chewed slowly. After a maddening length of time, she finally spoke. "We're going to talk about Dad."

"Your dad? What about him?"

Carla carefully blotted her lips with a napkin, then slowly folded it. She lifted her eyes to meet Suzanne's. "I don't want you to see him anymore."

The bite Suzanne was trying to swallow seemed to lodge in her throat. She took a sip of water and struggled to look calm. "Oh, really? Why don't you want me to see him?"

"Because if you keep seeing him, he might be stupid enough to ask you to marry him, and—" She stretched, then shrugged her shoulders. "I don't want you for a stepmother."

Suzanne stared wide-eyed. Anger, frustration, even fear, swept through her. Her heart pounded. What could she say? If she told this wild person it was none of her business, she might do something awful.

"See," Carla took a deep breath as though weary of

explaining. "We're happy just the way we are, Dad, Kristen, and me. Her voice was reasonable. "Nobody's going to take my mom's place." She narrowed her eyes and lifted her chin slightly. "Not you, or anybody."

Suzanne suppressed a gasp and managed to smile. "Come on, Carla. You don't expect your father to stay a widower, do you? Don't you love him? It's a lonely life."

"Stow it!" Her eyes popped wide with anger. "I'm warning you, leave my dad alone." She looked away from Suzanne, and her glance drifted to the service counter. All anger faded from her eyes as quickly as it had appeared. She twinkled a smile at the waiter. Then she turned back to Suzanne, shaking her head in mock sorrow. "I heard about your baby."

Suzanne's stomach lurched. "You did?"

Carla took another bite and chewed deliberately. "Next time Dad might not be around to save her."

Suzanne's hand trembled as she put down the pizza. She frowned at Carla and shook her head slightly. She had heard of jealous stepchildren, but this young woman had murder in her eyes. Suddenly it all seemed ridiculous, like a poor movie. She laughed aloud, a small, hysterical chirp of a sound. "Carla, you can't be serious. I told your dad yesterday that I wanted to be friends with you—"

"Forget it. I don't want your friendship. I don't want you, period. Stay out of my dad's life."

Suzanne seldom became out-of-hand angry, but it had happened a few times in her life. Once, when Del had pushed too far, and used too much sarcasm, she had thrown a lovely china cup into the sink, and gloried in the explosive crash.

She felt that insane destructive force now. She would have to get out of this person's presence or make a regrettable scene. She stood up, reached in her billfold and pulled out a five dollar bill. Her green eyes glinted down at Carla.

"I'm sorry you feel that way." She tossed the bill on the table. "But get this straight. I'll see your dad whenever he wants to see me." She whirled and almost ran out of the restaurant.

As she raced along the sidewalk to the office building, her mind churned with vindictive plans. She could call Vincent and tell him to do something with that brat, or there would never be a marriage. Better yet, tell him she wanted to get married now, as soon as possible. Las Vegas tonight would be fine. Move into the big house and tell her to get lost. In the elevator, she crumpled inside like a piece of paper. She knew she would do none of those things. She would do what she had to do: wait for Vincent to call her. Then, maybe she would tell him about Carla, but not in hate or anger. Together they would work out a plan to win her over. Tears threatened to spill out and she had to fight for composure as she stepped in the office.

Penny jumped up, ready to go to lunch. *At least she won't ask questions right now, thank goodness.*

As soon as Penny walked out, however, Justin came in and sat down in Penny's chair.

"Well, did you and Miss America get your business taken care of?"

Suzanne's smile was professional. "Oh, yes." She turned her back and frowned as she concentrated on her notes.

"I can't get over what a beauty she is." He raised his eyebrows and sighed.

And I can't get over how horrible she is.

"How old is she?"

Suzanne took a breath, turned and looked at him. *Old enough to take over the world.* "Nineteen— almost twenty."

"That's bad."

"Why?"

"Bad for me. I'm no cradle robber."

Suzanne couldn't keep the sarcasm out of her voice. "I don't think you need to worry."

"Really?"

"She has a three-year-old daughter."

"Divorced, huh?" He was almost grinning. "I'm going to call tonight." He stood up and clapped his hands. "I'll ask Marino if he cares if I date his daughter."

When Justin went back to his office a dreadful possibility entered her mind. *What if Justin does date her? And what if she can get him to fire me, to lessen the chances of my seeing her father?*

CHAPTER 12

THE NEXT WEEK was an agony of suspense for Suzanne. She was burning to know if Justin had dated Carla, but she was afraid it would be too presumptuous to ask. She became positive Carla would do whatever she could to get Suzanne out of the office. In the past two or three days, in fact, Suzanne was sure Justin had looked at her in a strange way.

Most of her thoughts, however, were about Vincent. Where was he? What was he doing? Why didn't he call? She ached to see him. Every time the telephone rang, whether at the office or home, there was a quick flare of hope. But he didn't call, and he didn't come into the office.

After ten days had passed and she still hadn't heard from him, she knew something was wrong. It wasn't beneath Carla to tell him some outrageous lie, but she felt sure he was too smart to believe it. No, something had happened to him. He was ill, or injured, probably near death in some hospital, and of course, Carla wouldn't call her. On the eleventh day, while Penny was at lunch, she called his office. After one ring she heard his rich voice. "Hello. This is Vincent Marino—"

"Oh, Vincent! Are you all right?"

"—I'm sorry not to be in the office at this time, but at the tone, if you'll leave your name—"

Suzanne hung up. She closed her eyes, leaned forward slightly, and hugged herself to keep from crying. She took a deep breath, then dialed his home number. She let it ring ten times, but there was no answer. She called twice more in the afternoon, even though she knew Penny might be able to hear the conversation, but there was still no answer. She asked the operator to verify that the line was still in service. It was. When Penny took her afternoon break she called his office again, but just as she was about to leave her number, Justin sprinted up to her desk with a document in his hand. She hung up quickly. *I'll try to call his home again tonight,* she thought. *When Harriet is watching the news, I'll call.*

That night after dinner Suzanne sighed and tapped her foot as she and Harriet washed the dishes. As soon as Harriet had put a dish in the dishrack Suzanne would snatch it up and whisk it dry. She tried to speed things up by bringing the utensils from the stove to the counter, but Harriet was not to be rushed. She seemed unusually full of cute things the children had done or said, and it was almost seven-thirty before Harriet went into the living room. As she settled in front of the TV, she called, "Suzanne? You coming in?"

"Be there in a minute." Suzanne put a squirt of lotion on her hands and rubbed it in. "I have to make a call first." As she picked up the phone a car door slammed, then the doorbell rang. She put the phone back. Who could that be? Holding her breath, and trying not to hope too much, she rushed to open the door. Her mouth opened. "Del!"

122

He was pale, and much thinner than the last time she had seen him. His suit coat hung on him, almost clownlike, and he hitched up his pants when he spoke. "Hi. Can I come in?"

As Suzanne stepped back, Randy shot out of the living room and into his arms. "Daddy!" He wrapped his legs around Del's waist and kissed his cheek. "Boy, I'm glad to see you." Suzanne's lips turned down. She had never tried to influence Randy against Del, but now she wondered how glad he would be to see his father if he knew that a few months ago he had chosen to leave them.

"I'm glad to see you, too." Del's voice was quavery.

"Son!" Wide-eyed and grinning, Harriet struggled out of the chair, then limped as fast as she could to kiss Del. "Welcome home."

When she tasted blood, Suzanne realized she was biting a hangnail. Squeezing that finger, she forced herself to be calm, but she could not bring herself to welcome Del. Besides that, she resented Harriet's verbal appropriation of the home. *It's mine, old girl.* She thought of the many nights Del had come home drunk, or failed to come home at all. And what about the other woman, the squandered paychecks, and recently, the absence of child support? *You'd better believe I've earned this house.*

Del put Randy down and drew a shuddering breath. "You're looking wonderful, Suzanne." He swallowed. Suzanne stared at his Adam's apple as it moved up and down.

"Thank you." Her mouth felt dry. She licked her lips. "You're, you're thinner."

He shrugged and frowned slightly. "I'm not feeling too super."

Harriet's toothy smile turned down. "What's wrong, son?"

He cleared his throat and reached out to touch the wall. "Do you mind if we sit down?"

Suzanne, standing with arms folded, nodded toward the living room and watched the responses of her family. Harriet guided him toward his big chair, but instead of crossing the room, he let himself down on the nearby couch. Harriet sat down with him, and put her hand on his forehead. Randy hopped up on the arm of the sofa, with his hand on Del's shoulder. Crystal surveyed her father from the middle of a circle of toys in front of the television. She didn't seem to recognize him, and after a moment's calm scrutiny, turned back to playing.

Harriet took her hand away. "You don't seem to have a fever." She frowned at him. "What's wrong?"

He closed his eyes briefly. "I'm not sure, Mom. The doctor at the center said for me to see my own doctor."

Suzanne eased down on a chair arm across from him and studied his features. Against his black hair his face looked white. There were lines she had never seen before. He looked old and sick. Some of her resentment faded, and while she had no affection for him, she did feel pity.

"I thought you were doing so well there," Harriet said. "What happened?"

Del nodded. "I was. I'd gotten completely over the withdrawal symptoms. I started eating better, and was even beginning to work out in their gym. Then one day I had a dizzy spell and fell down." Harriet gasped, and Randy's eyes became round. "I wasn't hurt, and I didn't tell anyone. But a couple days later I was walking down the hall and ran into an iron railing." He smiled, embarrassed. "That time I skinned my leg. Completely misjudged the distance."

"Del, that sounds serious," Suzanne said. "You'd better see Dr. Krueger in the morning."

Del shook his head. "No. Not yet. Nothing else has happened. I think I'm okay. I can't seem to eat very much, and I've lost more weight than I wanted to,

124

but . . ." He looked at Suzanne. His eyes were tortured. "I think my main problem is I'm homesick." Shocked, Suzanne watched tears form in Del's eyes, then run down his cheeks. A great, ragged sob shook his shoulders.

"Oh," Harriet whimpered. "My poor, poor boy!" She took his hand.

Randy blurted, "Please don't cry, Daddy. You're here now."

"Yes, honey, stay the night with us." Harriet was smoothing his hair.

Through half-closed eyes Suzanne looked at her husband, amazed at her own detachment. Yes, she was sorry for him, but she had no desire to hug him or comfort him in any way. After all, he had found another woman to comfort him. Where was she, now that he was sick? If he was sick. A slow anger began to burn inside. She had been outmaneuvered again. If he was really sick, or, even if he only said he was, Harriet would never forgive her if she didn't allow him to stay all night. She shook her head slightly as she watched Randy pat and caress his father. She couldn't refuse to have him overnight, not when Randy wanted him to stay. Her shoulders sagged. *You've won again, Del.*

She drew in a breath and tried to look pleasant. "Del?" He opened his eyes. "Would you like something to eat or drink? I mean, milk? Coffee?"

He smiled uncertainly. "Anything." He wiped his eyes. "Do you have any Coke? Anything would be fine."

Suzanne went to the kitchen. She leaned against the refrigerator, pressing her cheek against the cool door and looked at the telephone. Even if Vincent was home tonight, she couldn't call. She opened a bottle of Diet Coke, put ice in a tall glass, filled it, and took it in to Del.

"Well, Del," she said as she handed it to him, "I

125

guess you could sleep in Randy's room. He can sleep with me.'' Harriet's eyes widened and Suzanne turned away. "I'll put fresh sheets on the bed.''

"I'll help you," Harriet offered.

In Randy's room Suzanne yanked the bedding off and tossed it in a corner. Her lips were grim as she began to smooth on the fresh sheet.

"Suzanne, could you find it in your heart to—"

She glared at her mother-in-law. "Absolutely not! I know you love him, Harriet, but right now all I can remember is that he left me for another woman."

They finished the bed in silence. When they heard the front door open and close, both women rushed to the entry hall in time to see Del come back in, whiter than ever, lugging two suitcases. He looked away from Suzanne's shock and indignant eyes. Two suitcases? He knew he was going to stay! What happened to the girl friend? Had he already given up his condo? What gall!

She whirled away from him. "Randy!" Her voice was low and commanding. "Get in your pajamas, use the bathroom, then get in my bed." Her narrowed eyes didn't allow for any argument. She put Crystal to bed quickly, not allowing her to crawl away from the diapering even once, and without the usual tickling or story. When she snapped off the nursery light, she looked in the living room and spoke to Harriet and Del. "I'll be out of the bathroom as quickly as I can. Then I'm going to bed. Goodnight."

On Tuesday morning Suzanne was relieved that Del stayed in Randy's room until she left for work. She didn't want to talk to him. It had been all she could do to fend off Harriet's questions about the future without losing her temper. She had only slept about two hours all night long, and her body felt as though it had been beaten and wrapped in lead. The idea of Del being in the house, just a few feet down the hall, wondering if he was sick, wondering if he would go through with the divorce, interspersed with anxious thoughts about Vincent, had kept her in turmoil.

Under the fluorescent lights at the office, things seemed just as hopeless. She hated the thought of Del living with her, using the bathroom, eating with them. And what about money? Was he still working, or had he lost his job? Underneath and above all those thoughts, her heart ached for Vincent. She routinely uncovered her typewriter and unlocked the files.

"Did you bring your Bible?" Penny chirped.

Suzanne put a hand on her mouth. "Oh! No. I had it on the nightstand, too. I forgot all about tonight."

"You are coming, aren't you?" Penny's sapphire eyes begged like a puppy's. "Or can't you come again this week?"

Suzanne hesitated. She didn't want to go. She would much rather go home with the children. Then she remembered Del. He would be there tonight. She made up her mind quickly. "Yes, I'll go home with you, but let me buy hamburgers on the way, okay?"

After supper, Suzanne again followed Penny's green "bug" to the apartment house. She wrinkled her nose when she recalled how happy Harriet seemed over the phone when she told her about the Bible class. "That's fine, Sue. Stay as long as you want. Del and I have a lot to talk about. And he's getting acquainted with the children again." Then she had laughed. "He and Randy were having a big time at breakfast."

Yes, I'm sure they were, Suzanne thought. *Between Harriet and Del I won't rate at all with my kids. But I guess I ought to be glad she's in a good humor.* Suzanne felt it was a miracle that Randy had never said anything to Harriet about that Sunday at Vincent's. It was almost as though the boy wanted to close it out of his mind.

By the time they got to Penny's apartment, Suzanne was beginning to look forward to the sharing group. As before, John got there first, and this time, when Suzanne saw a certain expression in Penny's eyes when she looked at John, she knew what it was. It might not be love just yet, but it was definitely more than brotherly affection. The discovery pleased Suzanne. Over the past several months she and Penny had become quite close, and Suzanne had a genuine affection for her. Penny was sweet and good, and deserved the very best. Suzanne knew her broken engagement had hurt. Now it was evident she was thinking of a new love, too. *Oh, Vincent, where are you tonight?* She had tried again that day to reach his home, but there was no answer. Tonight, on the way home, she decided, she would stop at a phone booth and try to call him.

When the group had gathered, Suzanne recognized the girl beside her as the one who had asked the leader, John, to pray for her dog. Curious, Suzanne turned to her and asked how her pet was.

Dolly beamed with her reply. "Wonderful. The vet said he'd never seen such a quick recovery. I know it's the prayers."

John had overheard the question, and the chattering around the room stopped as he spoke and began the lesson. "Certainly." John's pale blue eyes sparkled. "One of the verses we'll study tonight tells us, if we stay close to Jesus, we can ask whatever we want, and He'll give it to us."

"Really?" Dolly's eyes were wide. "Where's that?"

"John 15." He flipped open his Bible. "Here it is. Verse seven."

Penny got her Bible and sat down on the floor beside Suzanne. She found the Scripture and held it up so Suzanne could see as John read it.

"If you remain in me and my words remain in you, ask whatever you wish, and it will be given you."

If only that could be, Suzanne thought, and then felt mortified. How could she even think about her possibility for new love when Del was in her house, this very moment, trying to make amends?

Someone was voicing her thoughts. "But John, that can't be true for everybody."

"The Bible is always true," he said. "Now let's look closely at that verse. Jesus clearly says we can ask whatever we want. But did you notice? There is a string attached: 'If you remain in me,' He says."

John looked around with a smile and continued. "Jesus knows every desire of our hearts. As a matter of fact, He has put the good desires there Himself. So if we stay close to Him and do as He tells us in the Bible, we can be sure we get what we ask."

Someone else raised a question, but Suzanne didn't hear. She was remembering a little neighborhood church. She was fourteen and understood for the first time that Jesus had paid for the time she stole the rouge from the drugstore, and that He had also paid for her many lies. He had been stretched out on a cross, so she could be sure of going to heaven. All she had to do, she was told, was be sorry she had done those things, and believe Jesus died for her. She had wept that morning, and walked up the short aisle to be one of those who accepted Christ. She really loved Jesus when she was a teenager. She even thought of becoming a missionary. What happened? When did she quit believing? Or rather, when did she begin to pretend she didn't believe?

"It's never too late to turn around," John was saying. "And when you are a Christian, you have Christ living in you, and you'll never be completely happy until you are following His will."

"What do you think of divorce and remarriage?" Suzanne blurted out. She saw Penny's head jerk up.

John smiled over at her. "All I can say, Suzanne, is that the Bible only gives one reason for divorce, and

129

that's adultery. In that case, as I understand it, it's okay to remarry."

Dolly spoke up. "I think it's only fair to be able to remarry if the divorce—for whatever reason—wasn't your fault."

John nodded. "God is always more than fair, Dolly. The thing is, He's a personal God, and each of us has to get our own individual answers from him."

"How do you do that?" Suzanne asked.

John motioned to his Bible. "That brings us back to the verse we were discussing: that if we're willing to live close to God, you know, sort of snuggle up to Him and invite him to share our lives, we can ask anything we want, and he'll give us answers."

Suzanne didn't hear much more of the Bible study. She was wondering what life would be like if she invited God to "remain" with her. Would He help her do the right thing even if that right thing were to restore a marriage with a man she no longer loved? She turned down the chocolate chip cookies and coffee, anxious to concentrate on her thoughts.

When she passed the shopping center she glanced at her watch. Nine-thirty. She turned quickly into the parking area and stopped near a public phone. She felt vulnerable and conspicuous as she walked up to the two-sided shelter with the phone hanging on it. What ever happened to phone booths, she wondered. She put in a dime, and by heart poked out Vincent's number. After the third ring a woman answered. "Hello? Hello?"

It didn't sound like Carla. Who was it? Breathing hard and suddenly afraid, Suzanne murmured, "Is—is this Carla?"

"No. Carla's gone to Palm Springs for a few days. Do you want to leave a message? I'm the house-keeper."

The housekeeper. With relief she asked, "Is Mr. Marino there?"

"No. He's out this evening, but he should be in shortly. He's gone to dinner with friends."

"Oh."

"Do you want to leave a message?"

"Uh, no. I'll call again. Thank you." She hung up quickly, biting her lip and fighting tears. So. He was well enough to be out with friends.

She walked slowly to the car and got under the wheel. She sat, almost in a stupor, and watched late shoppers. If she couldn't have Vincent she didn't see how she could go on. Yet she knew that divorce and remarriage were against everything she believed in. Maybe that's why she hadn't been able to reach Vincent. Maybe that was why Del had come back. Was God trying to give her answers? Even before she asked? She glanced at the empty seat beside her. Was God with her?

"God," she whispered, "Jesus, are you here? Am I a Christian?" Tears gushed down her cheeks. "What do You want from me? Is it my fault I love the wrong person?" Her throat felt strained, and there seemed to be no end to her tears. When she wiped her eyes she noticed a man staring at her through the windshield. Humiliated and angry, she started the Toyota, sped across the parking lot, partially missed the driveway, and bounced off the curbing.

By the time she reached home she had quit crying, but the sight of Del's car parked in the driveway underscored her almost hopeless situation. She parked behind him, locked her car, and started for the house. She hoped both he and Harriet were asleep. She didn't want to talk to anyone. Except God. Tonight she had to make the biggest decision of her life.

CHAPTER 13

As soon as suzanne stepped inside the darkened house, and saw only the glow from the night light in the bathroom, she let out her breath. *Thank goodness they've gone to bed*, she thought. She glanced down the hall and could see that Del had closed the bedroom door. That was a relief, too. She peeked in on Crystal, then tiptoed to her own room. She could barely see Randy's small shape under the covers.

Careful not to make any noise, she got her robe and gown from the closet, then glided into the bathroom and locked the door.

When she flipped the light switch, the mirror reflected her heartbreak. All her makeup was gone, her eyes were puffy, and her nose was red from crying. She took a deep breath and whispered, "Okay, God. This is it. I don't know what's happening in my life. But if You're trying to turn me around, I give in. Vincent doesn't want me anyway, and I guess Del does." She shuddered. "But I have to be honest with You. You know everything, anyway." Her expression turned fierce. "I don't want him. I hate him for being here. Is it wrong for me to feel that way?"

She wilted suddenly and stared down at the wash basin. "Lord, after all he's done to me I can't seem to help it." She looked up, above the mirror. "I'm so miserable. If there's anything You can do, I'd appreciate it, because—" She began to cry, and her shoulders shook. She almost choked as she struggled to suppress her sobs.

"Oh, God, You know I love Vincent, and I thought he wanted to marry me, but now . . ." She took a tissue and blew her nose as quietly as she could. "Is what John said true? About sharing our lives with You and then You'd answer our prayers?" She bit her lower lip, and looked in the mirror. With a trembling hand she pushed her hair away from her forehead, then slowly kneeled on the bathmat and closed her eyes. "I'm asking you right now to forgive me for all the years I've left you out of my life." Hot tears streamed down her cheeks. "I'll try not to do that anymore. And if You can possibly see Your way clear, please let me get back with Vincent."

With her eyes still closed she held her breath a moment and listened. She opened her eyes and looked around. Did she really expect an answer? She felt foolish, yet hopeful. She had just talked to God. Had He heard? She stood up, surprised that she had quit trembling. A tiny ember of hope glowed in her heart. Yes, God had heard.

Once in bed she snuggled up to Randy. Even though it was June, the nights were still cold, and she had been chilled through while using the outside phone. His body heat felt good to her, and she pulled him close. *My son, my darling little son. How I love you.* In the semi-darkness she raised up and looked at him. It occurred to her that God was looking down on her in the same way, loving her even more than she loved Randy. The thought brought tears to her eyes.

Although Randy was a wiggler and a flouncer in bed, Suzanne slept better that night than she had for a long time.

"I can't believe it's the end of June," she told Penny a few weeks later, as she prepared to close out the books.

"Me either," Penny grinned. "Hasn't this month been exciting, though, getting the computer, and you going to Bible class every Tuesday and . . ." She looked down at her left hand and touched a small sapphire ring. Her smile was tight, as though trying to keep from bursting with happiness. ". . .and John giving me this birthstone ring!"

"I'm so happy for you, Penny." Suzanne's smile was genuine. She wanted Penny to be happy, and although it was only a promise ring, Suzanne felt certain that John was the man Penny would marry. But she couldn't help comparing Penny's ideal romance to her own strange love life. Vincent had never called, or come to the office that she knew of, since that Sunday at his estate. And after she had learned on the phone that he was out with friends, she had never tried to call him again. It was over. She knew without a doubt, that humanly speaking, it had to be Carla's fault. Yet since she had turned her life over to God she became convinced it was His will for her not to see Vincent anymore. Jesus must not want her to remarry.

Accepting it was getting easier. There were times when she felt she couldn't stand another day without seeing Vincent, or at least talking to him, but she resisted the temptation to call. His wonderful face often appeared in her mind, and she was certain she would always love him. But life went on, and each day she thought of him with less pain.

One thing that was helping ease her heartache was reading the Bible. Following John's advice, she began to set the alarm half an hour earlier, and while everyone was still asleep, she would slip out to the patio to read and pray. The more she read, the more she wanted to read. She was astonished at the passages she chose. They seemed always to give her specific instruction and strength for that day.

Another reason it was getting easier not to think about Vincent, was the computer. It had been delivered and set up a few days after her phone call to his house, and in spite of hours of training from the computer company representative, Suzanne had struggled daily to understand it until gradually, the instructions and the processor came together, and she began to look forward eagerly to that part of her job. It filled her mind with new and challenging thoughts.

When occasionally her mind would rest from the computer an ever-present question popped up: What will the outcome be with Del living at the house? Everyday his presence there seemed to be more permanent. Only four days after he had come back, she came in from work that evening and was stunned to see him preparing dinner.

"Where's your mother?"

He was frying hamburgers and turned to face her, smiling. "She's back in her apartment." He flipped one of the patties. "I told her I thought it would be better for her arthritis to rest more. You know, Suzanne, that baby of ours is pretty hard on her." He ignored her open mouth and wide eyes. "Besides, I'll be on sick leave for another three weeks. I'll be glad to run things here for you."

"Why didn't you talk it over with me?" She glared at him, her eyes like emeralds in the sun.

He looked mystified, apologetic, helpless. "Why— it never occurred to me—"

"Nothing ever occurs to you." She ran down the hall to her room before she could say something she would regret.

By the time she changed into jeans and a shirt she had calmed down. After all, she told herself, no harm was done. He did know how to take care of his own children, and Randy adored him. Even Crystal was beginning to tag along behind him.

Now almost a month had gone by with the bizarre arrangement, and life at home was about as it had been with Harriet there. Suzanne usually cleaned up the kitchen in the evenings while Del played with the children and watched TV. After they were in bed, unless there was something special she wanted to watch, she would take her shower and go to her room and read a while. The first night Harriet was gone, Suzanne made up the couch for Randy.

"I can sleep there," Del had offered.

She shook her head. "It's not long enough for you. But Del, I want you to understand that this arrangement is only temporary. Randy needs his own room."

"Yes." His compelling eyes asked a question. She understood what he asked, but she had looked away.

Suzanne picked up the journal and accounting disc and sat down at the computer.

"How are things at home?" Penny asked as she flipped on the switches. Suzanne had finally told her about Del moving back. "Is he going ahead with the divorce?"

Suzanne's lips compressed as she shook her head. "I don't think so. The final petition has never been filed. Now he says it's up to me."

Penny's eyes were round. "What are you going to do?"

Suzanne shrugged. "What can I do? I didn't want the divorce in the first place. And now . . ." Her eyes slid away and focused on the floor. "Even if I did, I know what's in the Bible." She sighed and closed her eyes a moment. "We're supposed to stay married."

Penny frowned and chewed her lower lip. "Suzanne, I know you don't love him any more." She picked up a rubber band and stretched and twisted it as she talked. "Could you ask God to help you love him again? I mean, he isn't drinking, and you said he's—"

"Oh, Penny. I'm trying, but it's so hard. I don't feel like I want to love him. I want him out of my life." She was silent a moment and then added, "He's supposed to go back to work Monday."

"What'll you do with the children then?"

"Harriet said she'd come for awhile, but they both are pressuring me to quit this job."

"Oh, no."

"Don't worry. I'm not going to quit, at least for a while. I told Del, though, that if he didn't drink anything for six months, I would consider a reconciliation. Then I'd quit and stay home."

"Well, Suzanne, John and I pray for you every time we're together, and I pray for you when I'm alone, too."

"Do you really? Thank you very much. I need all the prayer I can get."

"I think it would help you all, too, if . . . if . . ."

Suzanne laughed, "If we start going to church."

Penny laughed. "Yes."

"I've already told Randy we're starting Sunday school this Sunday."

"You're kidding! Wait 'till I tell John."

"And I hope your nursery worker is the strong lady from the circus, because she'll be taking care of Crystal."

"Is your hus—is Del going?"

Suzanne looked prim and cold. "I haven't asked him."

Penny frowned. "Suzanne, he's no worse than the thief on the cross. And Jesus forgave him."

Driving home that evening after work Penny's words kept pelting her: He's no worse than the thief on the cross. *I know I'm supposed to forgive him, Lord, but then, he's never asked me to*, she rationalized, but then in the quiet of her mind she heard a response, a familiar voice that spoke into the depths of her being. *What if he doesn't ask? Will you forgive him anyway? Remember, Suzanne, I forgave you.*

Selena was out front watering her lawn when Suzanne got home. She locked the car, then walked over to talk to her neighbor. "Haven't seen you for ages, Selena." She paused. "How's Cheryl?"

"Hey, she's doing good in college! Ever since that night she took care of your kids, what'd you say to her, anyhow?" Suzanne lifted her eyebrows and shoulders innocently. "You must have influenced her someway because she's been like a different girl. She comes in when she says, and she's not so sassy."

"Good! So, what new project are you in the middle of now?"

Selena laughed. "Still trying to get the dumpsites cleaned up." She shook her fist and laughed again. "Someday we'll get the job done, too." With her other hand she waved the hose vigorously, as though she could force more water out. "What're you doing for fun, keedo?" She winked and lowered her voice. "I see the lord and master has returned."

Suzanne wrinkled her nose. "Yes. But it's not what you think."

"You're not back together?"

"He's living here, period."

"Why? Why you put up with something like that?"

"Because he says he's sick. But he won't go to a doctor."

"It's his drinking?"

"No. That I wouldn't put up with."

Selena frowned and pursed her lips. "Maybe that explains it."

"Explains what?"

"This afternoon he and Randy were playing ball out front on your lawn. I was working in that flower bed," she pointed to a rose garden between the two houses, "and all at once I saw Del run into the elm tree."

"You're kidding. When was that?"

"About a half hour ago. I stood up but I didn't want to say anything that would make him mad like he used to get. I thought he was drunk."

"Was he hurt?"

"I think the wind was knocked out of him, but by the time Randy got to him he was sitting up. Then he stood up and they went in the house. I don't think he even saw me."

Suzanne looked puzzled. "I'd better get in and see if he needs anything."

"Let me know if there's anything I can do," Selena called.

Crystal was in her play yard in the center of the living room, and Del and Randy were on the couch, watching a cartoon. Del, looking pale and exhausted, made an effort to stand when she came in.

"Keep your seat," she said. "Are you all right?"

"Sure." There was a quizzical expression on his face. "Why?"

"Selena said you ran into a tree, playing ball."

"So what? What a nosy old biddy." His laugh ended with a snort. "Couldn't wait to tell you, could she?"

"She just thought you might be hurt."

"Tell her, sorry, but I'm fine."

"Del, you don't have to be sarcastic. She didn't mean anything."

He glared at her, his eyes almost black as jet. It was the first time since he had come back that he had shown any sign of the old Del. It frightened her, and she wondered if perhaps he had been drinking. Her stomach churned as she went to her bedroom to change clothes.

During dinner Del seemed to have forgotten completely about his accident and Selena. He seemed tired, but cheerful, and asked polite questions about her day, and told her about the children. Once, when she warmed his coffee, she sniffed the air around his head, but couldn't smell alcohol. While cleaning up the kitchen she looked quickly through the trash, but found no beer cans, or any evidence of drinking. Yet his ugliness and sarcasm had seemed exactly as it used to when he was drunk. Maybe he had been drinking vodka or gin. She had heard they were supposed to be harder to detect on the breath. Whatever the cause of his behavior, it made her uneasy.

She would be so glad when he went back to work. She hated for the children to spend so much time with him, and the thought of their riding in the car with him, if he should drink, made her shiver. In bed that night she determined that tomorrow she would tell him, either he had to go see Dr. Krueger, or he'd have to. . . . *Have to what, Suzanne? Did you ask God for advice?*

Muffling her face in the pillow she cried, "Lord Jesus, I can't go on like this, hating him, afraid of him. Please do something. Protect the children." Then she remembered Penny's concerned question, and her whole body seemed to shrivel. With a groan she added, "Give me the heart to love Del again."

CHAPTER 14

ALTHOUGH DEL USUALLY stayed in bed until after Suzanne made breakfast for herself and the children, he was always dressed and in the kitchen, ready to take over when it was time for her to leave. This morning, however, it was nearly eight, and Del hadn't stirred. Suzanne looked at the clock almost every minute. She peeked down the hall and wondered if she should knock on his door. Tentatively, she took a few steps, then went back to the kitchen. Randy was stirring his cereal, playing some game that only he understood.

Suzanne sighed impatiently. "Sweetie, don't play with your food, okay? Why don't you go see why your daddy isn't up."

As she waited for him to come back, she took her keys out of her purse, sighed again, and tapped her foot. So far she had never been late, and since Justin was such a fanatic about it, she didn't want to antagonize him, especially now.

Randy walked slowly back to the kitchen and got in his chair.

"Well?"

"Daddy says he's sick to his stomach."

Anger blazed in Suzanne's cheeks. *Oh that's terrific. I couldn't smell it on him last night, but he's got a hangover, just like it used to be.* She hurried to the phone and dialed Harriet, who agreed to come right over.

Suzanne was two minutes late to work, but Justin was too busy to notice.

"He's talking long-distance," Penny mouthed, pointing at the light on the telephone.

"Whew." Suzanne grinned, then whispered her explanation for being late. "I don't know how sick he is—" she gave Penny a sharp look "—or from what."

"You mean—?" Penny made a drinking gesture.

Suzanne nodded slowly. "At least, that's what it seems like. I tell you, that man is driving me crazy." As soon as the words were out, her conscience jabbed her. *Didn't you ask the Lord to give you love for Del?* She compressed her lips and closed her eyes.

"Are you sick, too?" Penny sounded frightened.

Suzanne's eyes flicked open. "No, Penny. My conscience just struck me." She shivered and rubbed her arms. "I've asked the Lord to give me love for Del, but it isn't working."

"If you meant it when you asked Him, He will."

Suzanne shrugged, unlocked her desk and the files, and began to sort her work for the day. Justin seemed to get new clients every week. Even with the computer's help, Suzanne was inundated with work.

She intended to call Harriet on her ten o'clock break to see how she was getting along, but there wasn't time for coffee, much less a phone call. Justin had both phone lines tied up most of the morning, anyway.

"Suzanne?" Penny's soft voice penetrated her concentration. "Do you know it's ten minutes past your lunch hour?"

142

Suzanne looked at her watch and slumped. "I can't go right now. Why don't you take the early lunch today? I'll go when you come back."

Penny had only been gone a few minutes when the hall door opened. Vincent Marino stood there, thinner, but more handsome, more dear, even than in her dreams.

Involuntarily, she stood and took a step toward him.

"Suzanne!"

He seemed mesmerized, and for one long moment, love for her burned in his eyes. Then his lids half closed and his face hardened. "I thought this was your lunch hour."

"It's supposed to be." She came out of the gate and walked slowly toward him. "Why haven't you called me?"

He seemed startled, then angry. "Why haven't I called you? What do you mean? You told me not to."

Her eyes popped wide. "I what?" Her mouth hung open. "When?"

Frowning, he reached for his billfold. "I don't know what game you're playing, Suzanne." He took out a piece of buff colored paper that had been folded and refolded into a tiny square. He slowly opened it, then handed it to her. "Have you forgotten this?" It was a typewritten letter on office letterhead.

Bewildered, Suzanne took the sheet, and murmured the words, looking more amazed and indignant with each sentence: *Vincent, I've decided not to see you again. You're too old for me, and I do not like your daughter. My children don't like you, either. I'm glad I found out in time. You could never make me happy. Don't call me or try to see me, because my mind is made up. Suzanne Forrest.* The note was signed in a fairly good imitation of her own handwriting.

Suzanne shook her head back and forth in disbelief. "I didn't write this." His eyes narrowed. "Vincent,

143

you know I didn't write this. Look. The typing isn't from my typewriter. That isn't my signature."

Vincent pursed his lips as he took the paper and examined it. "Then who?"

"Carla! I should have known. She hates me."

"But the letterhead."

She glanced at her desk and snapped her fingers. "Did she ever tell you that she and I had lunch together?" He frowned, shaking his head. "The Monday after the children and I were at your house she came here to talk to me."

He folded his arms, the letter still between his fingers. "She never mentioned it."

"She came in around eleven-thirty. And just before lunch Penny and I were both in the rest room for a moment or two. She must have taken the stationery off my desk."

"This letter came in the mail on that Wednesday. Why did she want to have lunch with you?"

"To tell me to leave you alone."

"And you listened to her?"

"Yes and no. At that time I felt sure you loved me, and I told her I'd see you whenever you wanted to see me. But I also felt I couldn't come running to you to tattle on your daughter. So I kept waiting for you to call. At first I thought maybe you were sick, or had been called out of town. But after a couple of weeks went by, I believed you really didn't want me."

"After all I've said, how could you ever believe that?"

Suzanne pointed to the letter. "How could you believe I'd write that?"

He raised an eyebrow. "If you think back, Suzanne, I was always the one pushing for marriage." He swallowed, and smoothed the sides of his hair. "Besides, I probably am too old for you."

"Oh, Vincent." She stepped toward him, aching to touch him, to hug him, to press her lips on his.

He looked down into her eyes, then with a deep groan, he swept her into his arms. He murmured in her hair, "All these weeks."

She closed her eyes and rested her face against his neck. She could feel the heat of his flesh and smell the spicy aroma of his lotion. She wished she could stay in his arms forever, but after a short moment, he released her.

"Justin wants to see me about the trial date, but when I'm through with him, let me take you to lunch."

She gazed into his eyes, exulting in the love she saw there. Then she slowly shook her head. "We can't. I can't." She bit her lip and turned from him. "Del's living at home."

"What does that mean?" He spun her around. "Are you back together?"

"No." She shook her head violently. "But I may have to."

"You don't love him! You love me."

She nodded. "But there's something else." As she looked up at him her soul was in her eyes, willing him to understand. "I've turned my life over to God."

He studied her face a moment. "Does that mean you have to live with somebody you don't love? Somebody who left you for another woman?" He looked down at her. "Or do you really not want to be with me?"

She stamped her foot. "You know that isn't true! But, Vincent, the Bible says we're not supposed to divorce. If a man leaves his wife, she can't help that, but, don't you see? Del came back. He wants me now. He doesn't want to go through with the divorce." She blinked back tears. "And even if we get a divorce, the Bible says Christians aren't supposed to marry again except in the case of adultery."

Vincent's mouth tightened as he carefully refolded the letter. "I never believed you'd become a religious fanatic, Suzanne."

"Please, Vincent."

"Don't you know there are many ways of interpreting the Bible?"

"Yes, but it's very clear about that."

"If you take every word literally," he cut in, "you'd go crazy."

She let out her breath and looked up at him. "My darling, all I can tell you is that I love you more than I've ever loved anyone, but I've promised God to try and live by His standards."

He put the letter in his billfold, then looked at her with sad eyes. "What can I say?" He started toward Justin's office.

When Suzanne went back to her desk she was shaking. Losing Vincent, then discovering he still loved her, and then giving him up again, had been like shards of glass tearing at her heart. Yet she was experiencing a solid peace she had never known before. She had obeyed the Lord.

She looked at her watch and decided to call Harriet before Penny came back to let her know she would be a few minutes late. The phone rang fifteen times, but there was no answer. Alarmed, she opened her purse, got Selena's number, and pushed the tiny square telephone buttons.

"Selena?"

"Is this Suzanne? I was just about to call you."

"Why? What's wrong?"

"I've got Crystal over here—your mother-in-law and your ex, or whatever, have gone to the doctor's."

"How long will they be?"

"A good question. But I'm sorry to tell you, I have to be at a meeting at 1:30."

"My lunch hour starts in a few minutes. I should be there in less than twenty."

Why are you upset? she asked herself as she hung up. *You knew something was wrong with him. Be thankful he's gone to the doctor.* She realized, then,

146

that she had hoped his sickness was really a hangover, which would mean that the cure had failed. Then she couldn't be blamed for turning down a reconciliation. *Suzanne! How can you have such rotten thoughts, yet piously tell Vincent you've turned your life over to God? Oh, God! Forgive me.*

She stood up as soon as Penny came in, and picked up her purse. "Something's wrong at home."

Penny came through the gate and stood near her while Suzanne explained what had happened. "I've got to get home and see what I can figure out. Hope Justin will understand."

"He will." Penny waved as she walked out the door. "I'll pray."

Suzanne had just picked up the children from Selena's and walked in the house when she saw Del's car roll in behind the Toyota. She was shocked when she saw Harriet climb out from under the wheel. She hated to drive. Del was not with her.

Suzanne dropped Crystal in the play yard and rushed to meet Harriet. The woman was pale, and looked weak.

She reached out to her mother-in-law. "What happened. Where's Del?"

Harriet shook her head. "Let me sit down a moment." In the living room she sank into the nearest chair.

"Where's Daddy, Grandma?" Randy was leaning on her and talking right in her face.

"Get back, Randy. Let Grandma rest a minute."

"Del's in the hospital." Harriet blotted her forehead with a tissue.

"Hospital? Why?"

"He's there for tests." She kicked off her shoes. "Randy, dear, would you get me a drink of water, please?"

After Randy went to the kitchen, Harriet leaned toward Suzanne and spoke in a low tone. "Dr.

Krueger looked awfully serious, Suzanne. I'm scared.''

"What happened this morning?"

"After you went to work I went in to see if he wanted any breakfast, and he looked so bad. Said he had thrown up. It wasn't hard to talk him into going to the doctor." She clenched her teeth. "I drove him myself."

"Why didn't you call me?"

"I tried, two or three times, but those lines were always busy." She took a deep breath. "Anyway, it's not so far. The hardest part was finding a parking spot."

"Where is he?"

"Whittier. The doctor took him over and got him right in, like it was an emergency. That's another reason I'm scared."

Suzanne bit her lip and frowned. "Do you want to go see him tonight?"

Harriet's eyes were pleading. "Let me take care of the children, and you go see him."

After almost a week of tests, Dr. Krueger called Suzanne at the office. "I'd like to see you, Suzanne."

She left work right away, even though it was only midafternoon. She sat nervously, twisting her hands, waiting for the doctor to speak. Finally, he put down the report he had been studying, slipped off his glasses, and spoke directly.

"Suzanne, I'm sorry. It looks as though Del has a tumor on his brain. I'm afraid we can't operate."

She felt the blood drain from her face. She had known something was wrong with Del, but never dreamed it was anything this serious. She felt guilty for all the mean thoughts she had had about him. "What will happen?"

Dr. Krueger shrugged sadly. "It's a matter of time. Probably within a few weeks."

Without really seeing, she studied the doctor's glass-topped desk. How could she tell Harriet? And Randy? And what did it mean to her? She felt nothing. "Will he suffer?"

Dr. Krueger nodded. "We'll do all we can, but there's the nausea and headaches, and—" he looked keenly at her "—he may go blind. He'll need you, Suzanne."

Going to see Del at the hospital became part of her evening routine. The only night she didn't go was Tuesday. "I need that Bible study and prayer now more than ever," she told Penny.

All of July was hot. Every afternoon when Suzanne got in the Toyota she could barely touch the wheel, and even driving with all the windows down, and her hair blowing wildly, the car didn't cool down inside.

"Why don't you take Del's car?" Harriet asked. "It's got air conditioning." But for some reason, Suzanne didn't want to drive the Lincoln. Del had bought it without her even seeing it, and it had always been his car.

She had formed a habit of going directly to the hospital from work, visiting with Del until almost seven, then driving the six miles over Colima Road as fast as she could so she would have time to get Crystal and Randy ready for bed.

One night as she was driving home, she had a striking realization: God had answered the prayer to give her love for Del. At first she thought what she felt was pity because each day he became more pitiful. Some days he was rational, other days his behavior was peculiar. Her heart ached for him, a man who had once been so virile, now thin and listless.

When he was lucid she spoke to him about Jesus, and how He had died on the cross to take care of the mistakes they had both made. "Del, wouldn't you like for Him to be Your Savior? Then you'd never be alone, whether I'm here or not." He cleared his throat, nodded and whispered, "Yes." From then on she had begun to feel a tender love for him; not a romantic love, but a soothing love, a love that cancelled all her grievances against him.

Del's funeral was the first week in August. As she made arrangements, talked to his boss, spoke to the insurance agent, comforted Harriet and Randy, she felt a strength she knew came from above. Penny's church, which Suzanne now felt was her church too, also supported her with prayers, gifts of money, and food.

At the viewing, a young woman Suzanne didn't know, stood for a noticeably long moment at the casket, staring down at an almost unrecognizable Del. She stifled a sob and ran out the side door of the mortuary. *Del's former love?* Her thoughts flew to Vincent. She wondered if he had heard about Del's death. Sternly, she made herself put him out of her mind. Thoughts of another man at her husband's funeral seemed almost blasphemous.

CHAPTER 15

"GUESS WHAT?" PENNY'S EYES twinkled with mischief. Suzanne opened a desk drawer and began to lay out her work. Every morning it seemed Penny couldn't wait to start talking to her, especially since the funeral. It was undoubtedly a thoughtful effort on Penny's part to cheer her up. Sometimes, though, Suzanne wished she could lose herself in silence and work. It was hard to be cheerful and interested in anything any more.

She glanced up and smiled. "I give up."

Penny glowed with excitement. "Last night John took me to dinner at the Cattleman's Wharf."

Suzanne stopped sorting letters and looked at Penny with raised eyebrows. "Cattleman's Wharf! My goodness. What was the occasion?"

Penny waved impatiently. "My birthday, but—"

"Your birthday?" Suzanne looked dismayed. "Why didn't you tell me?"

"Wow, Suzanne. It's sure hard to talk to you sometimes."

"Well? When was it?"

"September tenth, day after tomorrow, but John isn't free that night, and I didn't want you to know because—"

"Didn't want me to know?" Suzanne made a note on her calendar. "I'm certainly glad I found out. I'm taking you to lunch, that is," she gestured toward Justin's office, "if he'll let us both off at once."

"You don't have to do that. Anyway, I want to tell you about last night."

"Right." She faced Penny with an intense look on her face.

Penny shook her finger and frowned. "And don't interrupt."

"You have my undivided attention, your highness."

"What happened was, we just got seated, and guess who I saw across the room?"

Suzanne shook her head and frowned in an exaggerated expression of suspense. "Who did you see across the room?"

"Our own Mr. Justin David Wheatley, with what's-her-name."

"What's-her-name?"

"You know! Mr. Marino's daughter."

Suzanne's smile faded. "You mean Carla."

"Yes! Carla. With Justin. They didn't see John and me, because they were only looking at each other."

"Hmm." Suzanne looked placid, but her stomach fluttered at the thought of Vincent. She still yearned for him, although she told herself everyday, "It's over." She hadn't seen him since she told him she was going to try to live by the Bible. She was almost certain he knew about Del's death through Justin. Although Vincent had carefully avoided coming to the office, she knew the two men often talked over the phone in regard to the trial, and they might have met for lunch, or after hours. It seemed apparent that he didn't want to renew their relationship. And, she reminded herself, even if Vincent did come back, she wondered if her new commitment to Jesus Christ would come between them.

". . . and so when I saw him pull out the little ring box—"

Suzanne snapped back to the conversation. "Wait a minute. What?"

Penny nodded. "You can imagine how I stared."

Suzanne's eyes were round. "Was it a diamond?"

"We weren't that close but whatever it was she looked pleased, and he put it on her ring finger."

Suzanne gazed down at the typewriter, shaking her head. A smile played at the corners of her mouth. Penny grinned at her. "What're you thinking?"

Suzanne blew imaginary dust from her typewriter keys. "Something naughty."

"Oh?" Penny looked guilty and eager at the same time. "What?"

"I was just thinking they deserve each other."

Both women were laughing when Justin rushed through the outside entrance. They choked back their smiles as he crossed the room.

"Good morning." He dazzled them with a big smile of his own. "Glad you're happy. Beautiful day." He breezed down the hall to his office.

As soon as he was out of sight they both collapsed in laughter.

Wiping her eyes, Suzanne whispered, "And he never saw you last night?"

Penny shook her head. "If he did, he didn't act like it. I'm sure he didn't know we were there."

"I guess our boss is in love."

A few minutes later, seated in a chair opposite Justin, with her notebook open and pen poised, she waited for him to start dictating. He cleared his throat, and she looked at him.

"Susie, since you're so much older," he grinned when she scowled at him, "I thought you might give

153

me some advice." His green eyes met hers and for the first time since she had known him, she saw a softness, a vulnerability that surprised her. "Suzanne, I'm in love, really in love." She stared at her notebook and waited for him to go on. He leaned back in his chair and rubbed his chin. "I'd like to know what you think. Is ten years too much difference in age?"

She thought of Vincent and shook her head. "Not if you both love each other."

"I love her." He shook his head as though to clear it. "She's made me crazy." He laughed softly, adoringly. His smile gradually faded. "But what if I am too old? What if she gets bored with me?" He looked sharply at Suzanne. "You know who it is, don't you?" To her relief he didn't wait for an answer. "It's Carla Marino, Vincent's daughter." He closed his eyes and drew air to the bottom of his lungs, then let it out in a rush. "I've been off balance since that day she came to have lunch with you. I think she loves me, too. At least she accepted a ring last night."

"You mean a diamond?"

"Yes, ma'am. A diamond."

"Well, then. She must love you."

"And you don't think I'm too old?"

Her eyes focused on one of the photographs behind him as she thought of the Carla she knew: selfish, willful, hot-tempered. "I don't think your age will be a problem." She traced her pen along the spiral wire of the shorthand pad. "In fact, it may be an asset." She paused a moment. "Does Mr. Marino know?"

Justin nodded shortly. "He knows. I don't think they're on very good terms." He pursed his lips and frowned. "I think he'd be glad to get rid of her."

"Justin!" In spite of the rebuke in her voice, she was amused at him.

"I'm serious. I think he likes the housekeeper better than his own daughter."

· "The housekeeper?" She frowned. *Nell?* She had never met her, but she had a mental picture of a gray-haired lady in her late sixties. A strange fear chilled her. "Why do you say that?"

"Every time I go to get Carla, they're always together."

Suzanne's expression didn't change, but a dull pain began somewhere near her heart. *It's over, Suzanne.* She forced herself to think of something else. "Have you met Carla's child?"

Justin grinned and his green eyes glinted. "Kristen? Yeah. She's a little doll."

Suzanne did a double take. *A doll? Love is blind.* "Have you thought how it would be to have a ready-made family?"

"Sure. It'll be great. I'll have two dolls around the house."

Suzanne smiled. "By the way, Justin. This is off the subject, but, I was wondering if you'd ever told Vincent about my husband dying?"

He frowned and tapped his pursed lips with an index finger. "Hmm. I can't say that I did, Susie. I don't remember it, anyway." He looked apologetic. "I guess I never thought of it. When I'm with Carla I'm pretty self-centered." He shrugged and smiled. "Should I have?"

"Oh, no. I just wondered." Her mind tried to process this new information. If Vincent didn't know about Del, how could he know she was available? *But Suzanne,* she told herself, *you are not available to an unbeliever.*

"You dated him a few times, didn't you?"

She nodded. "But there was nothing—lasting."

"Could there have been, if your husband hadn't come back?"

"I don't know. We had different opinions on several things."

"Too bad. You ought to try to get together. He's a

good catch for some woman." He gave her a wise look, then leaned forward. "Well, Ms. Counselor, since you don't think this dude is too old for Princess Carla, maybe I can put it out of my mind now and get to work."

For the next two weeks Penny often remarked to Suzanne how different their boss had become.

"He's always been nice to us," she said, "but now it's like he's sort of . . ." She looked up at the light fixture and twisted her mouth, ". . . cuddly."

Suzanne laughed. "I wouldn't go that far. But he does seem softer. People in love are always sweeter." She winked at Penny. "Except you. You've always been sweet."

Penny lifted her chin, teasing. "Who says I'm in love?"

"Nobody has to. On Tuesday evenings a blind person could tell you and John love each other."

Penny looked pleased, and her face got rosy. "It's true. I do love him."

"I'm glad. Think what a wonderful world it'd be if everyone had someone to love."

A lump formed in her throat. She had never been so lonely in her life as she had been the past month. Before Del died she had been on an endless treadmill, going to work, then the hospital, then duties with the children. Most nights she was exhausted when she went to bed. After he died, there was still a lot of activity, her job, as well as some kind of widow-related business to attend to almost everyday. Now that everything had been settled, even though she was still busy with her job and the children, she felt empty, and had a lot of time to think. With both Justin and Penny in love, her loneliness seemed to be magnified. There was nothing to look forward to. She had to get through fifteen waking hours everyday, then start it all over again.

She realized, however, that she was looking forward to Vincent's trial date, set for the last Thursday in September. She had even bought a new dress to wear that day. At least she would see him for a few minutes, and maybe talk to him about Del's death. *But for what purpose?* The Bible was as clear about that as it had been about divorce: "Do not be yoked together with unbelievers." John quoted that Scripture almost every week at Bible study, and it always made her miserable.

However, the Bible study was one bright spot in her week, and since she had started going to church, she looked forward to Sunday morning, too. She had met several "singles," both men and women, and while she was pleasant to them, she hadn't allowed herself to be drawn into any of their activities. One man, tall, homely, and slightly balding, had invited her and the children to "McDonalds for hamburgers" one Sunday, but she had gently said, "Another time, perhaps."

"Justin may not be cuddly," Penny said, looking at the tiny sapphire ring on her third finger, "but he's definitely nicer. He even noticed this ring the other day. But guess what? John's going to buy me a diamond for Christmas."

"That's wonderful, Penny." Suzanne glanced at her own wedding set. She had started wearing the rings when Del went to the hospital, and for some reason had never taken them off. *I ought to sell them,* she thought. *And Del's car, too.* "When do you think you'll get married?"

"Probably next June."

"Nothing wrong with a June wedding." Her face was animated, but her mind wasn't on Penny's wedding date. She was counting the days now, until Vincent's trial date.

The afternoon before the trial Justin brought in some letters he had signed. He placed them on her desk then blew his breath out, making his cheeks look like small balloons. "Well, girls, oh, excuse me; I mean ladies."

"Ladies?" Penny gave him a warning look.

"I mean women."

"That's better." Penny said laughing.

"What I was going to say is, if you don't mind . . ." he coughed, put his hands in his pockets, then took them out again. "Would you say a good word to the Man upstairs for me tonight? The Marino trial tomorrow is going to be hard." He shifted from one foot to the other. "T. Morgan Tillman is a brilliant attorney, especially in this kind of a trial." He folded his hands together and looked mournfully up at the ceiling. "I'm going to need all the help I can get."

Penny's face was a picture of concern. "I'll pray, Justin." She nodded confidently. "He'll take care of it."

"I certainly hope so." He started to walk away, then came back. "Susie, in the morning will you call that Gladys whatever her name is? The one that wants to sue her daughter?"

Suzanne nodded. "Gladys Petry."

"Set up an appointment next week. I forgot I won't be here in the morning."

Suzanne's mouth opened slightly. "But I thought you and Mr. Marino would both be here in the morning, before the trial?"

"Oh, no. It'll be easier for him to drive out to Pomona from his house, and I have an earlier case, *Garcia* v. *Beckenridge*. Remember?"

Suzanne felt caved in, as though she had been hit in the stomach. She didn't hear anything else Penny or Justin said. A dream she had been building for weeks had just dissolved. She wouldn't get to see Vincent tomorrow after all.

At home that evening, she went through her duties in a mental fog. Her disappointment was so great it was all she could do to keep from crying.

She tried to mask some of her melancholy by playing hard with the children, and she read an extra long story at bedtime. She even watched an old Burt Reynolds movie with Harriet so she wouldn't have to think, or answer questions. At last it was time to go to bed, but she couldn't sleep.

She sat up, turned on the bed light and tried to read the Bible, but the words didn't make sense, and what she did understand, she didn't want to hear. Unshed tears made her eyes ache, and she could feel her mouth turn down in self-pity. She closed the Bible with a snap. "I thought when I turned everything over to You I'd be happy," she whispered. "But things are worse for me than they've ever been. Vincent doesn't love me. He's even interested in his housekeeper. Penny's engaged. And Justin, who doesn't give a fig for Christianity, is in love and happy. I thought You cared for me. The one thing I've been looking forward to, You've denied."

Tears slipped down her cheeks. For several minutes she reviewed every poignant and precious memory of Vincent, crying silently and so much, she had to get out of bed to get more tissues.

She finally wiped her eyes and blew her nose for the last time. There were no more tears. She sighed a deep, shuddering sigh. She couldn't dredge up anything else to cry about. Her nose felt swollen, and she couldn't breathe through it.

She began to feel ashamed of her outburst to God. Hadn't he said, "Do not be yoked together with unbelievers"? She knew that. So why had she been looking forward to seeing Vincent? Why was she hoping to be with him again, when he had told her she was a fanatic for believing in the Bible? Hadn't she told God she would go His way? *But, Lord, I love him so.*

Then she began to think of Penny, what a sweet friend: the Bible study, the fellowship at church, and above all, her relationship with Christ. She couldn't have that fellowship and Vincent, too. She was against a stone wall.

"Suzanne," she whispered. "Quit pretending. Say it's finished, and mean it."

She got out of bed again, this time to drop to her knees, "Lord, I've been kidding myself. Forgive me for all the things I said a while ago. I do love You. With your help, I won't ever try to see Vincent again."

CHAPTER 16

SUZANNE AWOKE WITH a heavy heart. Her first thought was, *it's over. No more Vincent. Not ever.* "Oh, God. Help me get through this day," she cried silently.

As she made her bed, she remembered a remark John had made one night at Bible Class: "God never promised it would be easy. It's hard to live for Christ."

Dragging, she made herself get ready for work. In her slip she stood in the closet, staring at her new dress. It was a shirt dress, thin crepe, with narrow green and white stripes. The green brought out the color of her eyes, and the style was good on her. She pressed the silky material to her lips. *I got it for Vincent*, she thought. *How can I ever wear it?*

Suzanne, do you love him more than Me?

Her eyes widened and she let go of the dress. *No, Lord!* Did God want her to wear it? Hesitantly, she took the dress off the hanger, then put it on and buttoned it. As she fastened the belt she looked in the mirror. The dress was perfect for her. She closed her eyes. *Lord, I'm going to wear it for You.*

A rush of pleasure, a warm, sparkling joy, shimmered through her. As she brushed her coppertone hair, she discovered she was "whoosh-whistling" one of the choruses she had learned at Fellowship. The tune lilted around in her mind all the way to the office.

At work she suffered a temporary setback when she unlocked the office door and realized she was alone. Penny had an early dental appointment and wouldn't be in until 9:30, and Justin was already in court. As she stood in the center of the silent reception room, she remembered the hope she had had for this day. When she felt tears begin to form she stamped her foot and shouted, "No!" She marched through the gate, tossed her bag in a drawer, and yanked off the typewriter cover.

She sat down at her desk, and as she laid out her work for the day she gradually felt a new enthusiasm for her job began to assert itself. She had always liked working for Justin, but ways to become more efficient began to spring up in her mind. For one thing, why not enroll in the next computer class offered in night school? If she knew more about the thing, she could take on more responsibilities, and perhaps teach Penny as well.

At the rate Justin was building clientele, he would probably be taking on a partner soon, so it would be important for Penny to know more. He might even hire another person to do office work. In that case, she would need to know something about office management. There was no end to the possibilities of this job. She felt excited, and determined she would do the best she could.

She hummed as she worked, feeling happier than she had for a long time.

When Penny came, looking pale, Suzanne smiled compassionately. "You okay?"

"I guess." She came through the gate and put her purse on the desk. "You seem happy. I heard you humming. What's up?"

"Nothing. What'd the dentist do?"

Penny made a face. "I have to go back and have a wisdom tooth pulled."

Suzanne winced. "I sympathize."

"I love that dress. Why are you so dressed up?"

"I don't know. Maybe to celebrate my new image."

"What new image?"

"You know. My new life with Christ. Doesn't the Bible say something about being a new person?"

Penny looked at Suzanne with love and pride in her eyes. "Yes. 'If anyone is in Christ, he is a new creation; the old has gone, the new has come.'" She put a finger to her forehead, "Second Corinthians five-seventeen."

"Bravo! I don't know too many Scriptures by heart yet, but I will."

The telephone rang and Penny pushed her long hair away from her ear to answer. "Justin Wheatley's office." As she listened she signaled with her eyes to Suzanne. "Oh, sure, Justin. Just a minute." She pushed the yellow hold light. "For you."

"Hi, Justin." She had a pen in her hand ready to write.

"Susie, you're not going to believe this, but I left a brief on my desk."

She tittered. "I don't believe it. Not you."

"I told you Carla has made me crazy. Anyhow, if you leave right now you should be here in twenty-five minutes, barring freeway traffic. That'll just give me the time I need to review it before court's in session, okay?"

"Wait a minute. Let me be sure it's there." She put the phone on hold and ran to his office. The folder was in the center of his desk. When she read *Marino* v. *Homeowners* on the label she closed her eyes for a moment, and began to tremble inside. She would see Vincent after all! She picked up the phone, suppressing the wild excitement that was exploding within. "It's here, Justin."

I'm here, too, Suzanne.

"I knew it was. I'm not that far gone. So let's quit talking, and you get going, okay?"

She put the phone back in position, picked up the folder and almost ran to her desk.

"I have to go to Pomona." She got her purse and waved at Penny. "Hold the fort."

Suzanne glanced at the sky as she ran to her car. Tan-grey smog hung over the basin, partially blocking out the sun, yet the air was hot and sticky, and smelled like carbon-monoxide.

Inside, the Toyota felt like an incinerator as she drove toward the freeway. She picked up speed, and with both front windows down, the interior cooled a couple of degrees. *What a mess I'll be by the time I get there. Hair blown to pieces, and sweating. My new dress!*

By the time she passed the Azusa off ramp the car was cool enough to roll up the window on her side, which cut out some of the wind and noise. She took a few deep breaths and tried to relax. It seemed strange to be out during the day. She glanced at expensive homes, high up on flowering hills, and wondered if the people who lived in them were happily married. She thought of Vincent's beautiful estate, and what married life might have been like with him. She immediately brushed away the thought. She had promised *Him.*

She made herself think about her own home; Crystal, she would be two in a few months, and Randy. Randy. Another worry. He had been happy in kindergarten, but now, just two weeks into first grade, his teacher had informed her he was a problem. *He needs a father. Suzanne! Don't do this to yourself. You're trusting God now, remember?*

I'm trying to fight it, Lord! Her hands were sweaty as she gripped the wheel and stepped on the gas to pass a car. But instead of speeding up, the car began to slow. She pressed the pedal all the way to the floor, yet the car continued to lose power. Other drivers began to veer around her, mouthing insults. Frightened, she made her way to the outside lane, and then to the shoulder, just as the station wagon rolled to a stop.

She turned off the key and sat hunched over the wheel. *Now what?* She glanced at her watch. Justin was expecting her in twelve more minutes. She turned the key, but the starter only growled. Trucks, cars, vans, hundreds of vehicles sped by. Everyone was moving except her. *Help, Lord. What am I going to do?*

How far was the nearest phone? She began to breathe too fast, partly from anxiety and partly from the heat, which was crowding in on her, stifling, unbearable. She rolled down her window, and was blasted by even hotter air as a semi-truck roared by a few feet away.

She had to get to a phone. She rolled up the windows again and reached for her purse. As she opened the door she saw a sports car skid across two lanes of traffic, scream to a stop on the shoulder, then back up and stop.

Vincent leaped out of his Porsche and ran the few steps to her.

"What's the matter?" He was frowning as he shouted. Relief made her weak. She could only shake her head and shrug. He was beside her now. He glanced at his watch. "I'm due in court in less than half an hour. Lock it up, and come on."

She grabbed the folder and with trembling fingers, locked the station wagon, then followed him to the Porsche. How big he looked, sprinting ahead to open the right side of the car. He wasn't wearing a coat, and his white shirt seemed blinding in the hazy sunlight. Wordlessly, she got in as he held open the door. He raced around to the other side and in seconds he was beside her, threw the car in gear, and roared down the freeway.

He spoke without looking at her. "Where were you going?"

She lifted the folder so he could see the name. "Justin forgot it. I'm supposed to be there in three minutes."

He stepped harder on the accelerator and moved to the inside lane. "I can't work miracles, but it beats what you had." There was no mirth in his tone, no smile on his lips.

It took all her willpower to quit staring at him. How dear he looked. *Help me!* Aloud she said, "I didn't mean to complain. I'm so grateful you happened along, and were willing to stop."

"You'd have been cooked if you'd stayed in your car." She nodded, breathing in the cooled air. She felt a trickle of perspiration on her temple, and smoothed back her hair. "I must look awful."

"You're thinner." He flicked a glance at her. "But you look good. If you want to comb your hair there's a mirror on that visor."

Self-consciously, she opened her purse and found a comb, then timidly pulled down the sunshade. Her hair was damp and tangled, and her face was still flushed from the heat. She combed her hair and put on gloss, aware that he was glancing at her. She closed her purse and turned her face toward the window.

"Seeing you on the shoulder was what you'd probably call a miracle."

She faced him. "What do you mean?"

"I intended to leave a half hour sooner this morning, and I usually get on the freeway further east, but I had a call from a new supplier, and he wouldn't deliver a load of lumber without a purchase order, so I had to take it to him." A tight smile appeared for a moment on his lips. "Isn't that what you'd call a miracle?"

Suzanne smiled weakly. "I guess so. I know I'm certainly thankful." She saw they were in the city of Pomona now, and soon her time with him would be over. Justin wanted her to stay at court, so most likely she would ride back to the office with him.

"How's remarried life?"

Suzanne cocked her head. "Pardon?"

"Married life? Are things working out?"

Her lips parted and she blinked. "You really didn't know?"

"Know what?"

"Del died August second."

Vincent's head snapped around to stare at her, and he almost missed the Garvey turnoff. "I didn't know." His brows drew down. "That lawyer never said a word."

"It doesn't matter."

"Of course it matters. You need all your friends at a time like that. I know."

Friends? Is that how you think of me? "Everything is working out, Vincent. I have a good job, and I have," she glanced at him, "I have the Lord. That's all I need."

His jaw line tightened. "I find that hard to believe. God made male and female, and He meant for them to be together." He was going almost too fast when he turned into the courthouse parking lot. "Even I know that. Nell and I have—"

"Oh, look! There's Justin." She waved as they went by him. "He looks frantic."

"Probably is." He wheeled into a small parking space and looked at his watch. "My case starts in fifteen minutes."

Suzanne picked up her bag and the folder, and got out before he could put on his coat and come around to open the door. *What had he just said about Nell? 'Nell and I.'* She trotted along beside him, trying to keep up. Justin had inferred that he was more interested in Nell than his own daughter.

Justin began to yell as soon as they came in sight. "Man, you two have had me in knots. Where's your car? Never mind. Let's go." He grabbed the brief and the three of them ran for the elevator.

In the courtroom Suzanne sat in the front row of chairs, while Justin and Vincent took their places in front. Her heart pounded as the bailiff called Vincent's case. The trial was short, and although T. Morgan Tillman was as brilliant as Justin had predicted, the evidence in Vincent's favor was convincing. The judge removed all restrictions from the property, and awarded Vincent almost all they had asked in damages.

After the decision, both Justin and Vincent were jubilant and wanted to celebrate.

"Let's stop at the Velvet Turtle on the way in," Justin suggested. "I'm starved."

"Fine. And it's on me." Vincent grinned, showing his even, white teeth. "Good job, Wheatley."

In the parking lot Justin touched Suzanne's shoulder and pointed. "My car's over there."

Vincent stepped toward her. "She came with me, so I'll see her home."

Once in the car Vincent was almost giddy, "I can't believe that hassle's over."

Suzanne grinned and nodded. "And didn't that homeowner's representative look mad when the judge gave his decision?"

Vincent laughed again and slapped his leg. "Serves him right, after what he tried to pull."

Suzanne sobered as she looked at his profile. *We're laughing and talking together as though we've never been apart.* She turned away from him. "Oh, dear." She pointed across the divider. "There's my car."

He patted her hand, and it was like an electric current. "Don't worry about it. I'll send the auto club for it."

"I can't let you do that."

"Of course you can. It's my fault you had to drive in this heat. Your car needs work. I told you that before."

"But—"

"Hush. Here's our turnoff."

In the Velvet Turtle, Suzanne was almost overcome with nostalgia, and had to struggle to keep from crying. It seemed like yesterday she had fallen in love with Vincent in this place. The waitress brought water and menus.

He touched her hand again. "Please, order more than soup." Her eyes sparkled and she smiled inside. *He remembers, too.* "Justin, if you want something to drink, don't let me stop you."

Justin winked at Suzanne. "Vincent tells me he's a teetotaler now. Even went to church last Sunday."

Suzanne gasped at Vincent.

He grinned. "It's true. In fact, I've gone to Nell's church twice." He gave her a guarded look. "A while back a friend of mine said she was going to try to live by the Good Book. I thought it was baloney, but I decided to see what it had to say. So Nell and I've been looking into it, almost every evening."

He was reading the Bible! Hot tears popped up in her eyes and threatened to spill. "It's nothing to cry about." His eyes twinkled as he looked across at Justin. "It's really an amazing book, Counselor. You ought to read it."

Justin closed his eyes briefly, then signaled the waitress. "Maybe I should have a drink."

Suzanne gazed at Vincent, wonder in her eyes. "You went to church." Her face was luminous. "I'm so glad."

He looked down into her eyes for a long moment. "I'm glad, too. Nell's church is different than the one I was brought up in, but I've learned quite a bit in just two Sundays."

Nell again! What is she to him?—not that it matters—but I have to know.

169

Vincent closed his menu. "I'm beginning to see things differently, especially the things we talked about."

When the waitress came to take their orders, Justin ordered a margarita. He looked at Suzanne and Vincent, and shook his head. "Better make it strong," he added.

He's seeing things differently—does that mean he believes? She forced herself to look away from his eyes. "Vincent, I didn't get to meet Nell. What's she like?"

"Nell? She's a wonderful big Irish lady, not bad looking. Probably old enough to be my mother. Why?"

Suzanne smiled slightly and raised an eyebrow at Justin. He shrugged sheepishly.

Vincent looked at him, then at Suzanne. "What's going on?"

Before Suzanne could answer, Justin blustered, "I was kidding around one day and told Susie that you were interested in your housekeeper."

"What?" Vincent stared at him, then laughed. "If I'd known that I'd have kicked you out of the house!" Vincent leaned toward Suzanne. "No, dear lady, I haven't had any interest in anyone since the day we had lunch right here." She glanced at Justin and felt herself blushing. "I told you before I want you for my wife, and I'm glad to have a witness when I ask you once more. Will you marry me?"

CHAPTER 17

"VINCENT!" SUZANNE LAUGHED TO HIDE her embarrassment, and tried in vain to collect her spinning thoughts.

Justin looked up at the ceiling. "Good grief," he moaned.

"What now, Counselor?"

He shook his head. "I'll probably be the only lawyer in the Bar Association whose secretary is his mother-in-law."

"You don't have to worry about that, my boy." Vincent buttered a roll, and gave Justin a knowing wink. "My wife will stay at home and take care of me."

"Susie, say no to this man, okay?" Justin looked pitiful. "You and I are a good team. I don't want to break in a new secretary."

"Put your mind at ease, boss." Suzanne answered smoothly. The talk about marriage both delighted and frightened her. Just last night she had told the Lord she would never try to see Vincent again, and here she was, experiencing thrill after thrill. *And, Lord,* she beamed inside, "You arranged it all."

After lunch, Justin stood up abruptly. "Susie, why don't you take the rest of the day off."

"Are you sure?"

He nodded as Vincent stood, and extended his hand, "Thanks again, Counselor."

Justin laughed. "You may change your mind when you get the bill."

When he was out of sight Vincent sat down and gently took Suzanne's cold hand in his warm one.

"I'm sorry if I embarrassed you a while ago. But now that I know you're free—and I still can't grasp it!" His voice was soft, and his eyes seemed to have fire in them. "But you are free. I ask you, once more, to be my wife."

She closed her eyes and bit her lip. Her eyes were sad when she looked at him. "Vincent, don't ask that. I can't marry you."

He put his finger gently on her lips. "I know. Don't say anymore until I tell you something."

He took both her hands, and kissed the palms. Suzanne trembled at his touch. *I can't fight this alone, Lord. Please be with me.*

"Darling, a week ago in church, Nell's preacher made me understand for the first time that belonging to a big church didn't mean anything, unless you belonged to Jesus Christ." Suzanne held her breath, afraid to move for fear she would awake and find she was dreaming. "He asked me if I believed Christ died for my sins." Vincent chuckled. "I said, 'Sure, He died for the sins of the world.' But that wasn't the answer this preacher wanted. He said, 'Vincent, Christ died for your sins. Can you accept that?'" He paused. "Suzanne, I did."

Suzanne's eyes were wet. "I can't believe this is happening. I can't believe it."

"Believe it. Last Sunday I went into business with the Lord Jesus Christ." He put his arms around her. "And you were the first person I wanted to tell, but I thought you were still married."

172

She rested her head on his shoulder, unmindful of the waitresses who passed and flashed knowing glances at them. Vincent, a Christian. A hopeless dream come true. *Oh, thank You, Lord.*

"Now you'll marry me, won't you?" Vincent kissed her eyelids. As his lips moved toward hers she pulled away and looked up at him.

"What about Carla?"

He sighed and released her. "We almost had a complete falling out over that letter. She admitted the whole thing. While you and Penny were in the rest room she took the stationery, just like you said, and used a typewriter at the library."

Suzanne looked out across the dining room. "She must hate me. How can we ever be happy with her feeling like that?"

"Listen, first of all, I think I scared the— whoops!—the daylights out of her. I threatened to have her hauled into court for defamation of character. Your character." He smiled. "I couldn't have made it stick, but I think she was scared. And, I told her she wouldn't enjoy living in a one-room apartment either."

"You'd never do that."

"Well, maybe not. But I took her car and credit cards away from her for a month." He tipped up his cup and drank the rest of his coffee. "The best thing that's ever happened to her is the Counselor. I think she's as much in love with him as I am with you, and it's changing everything."

Her expression was dreamlike as she looked in his eyes. "Justin is mad, absolutely mad about her, too. He's really a nice fellow."

"He's a great attorney. But I want to share a secret. I think he did a good job for me today, but you saw that other lawyer. He was formidable. I believe the reason the judge decided in my favor was be- cause . . ." He swallowed, then pointed up. "I talked to Him about it."

Suzanne took one of his big hands in her small ones, and held it to her lips for a long time.

With his lips against her hair he whispered, "When shall we get married? Tonight, in Las Vegas?"

"No. I want to be married in church. But, Del has only been gone two months."

"You didn't love him, did you?"

"No, but I love his mother, and I think it would be the right thing to wait."

"Not a year. I can't face that." He sighed and looked across the room.

She touched his face so he would look at her. She loved him more than ever, but she was growing up in Christ. "Let's take one day at a time. Today, glorious day, we have each other again."

"Suzanne, my Suzanne." He crushed her in his arms and kissed her deeply, as though trying to make up for all the time they had been apart. And even the wait before them could not crush the joy in Suzanne's heart. Joy in the goodness of the Lord, and the new love He had given her.

ABOUT THE AUTHOR

MAB GRAFF HOOVER is a romantic person who loves writing romance novels. Born in Parsons, Kansas, Mab now lives in Bellflower, California, with her much-adored husband. She is a homemaker, mother, grandmother, and a full-time writer.

Mab has written several inspirational books for Zondervan, including *God Loves My Kitchen Best*, and *God Even Likes My Pantry*. On writing, she says, "It's good to dwell on happy and light thoughts." Although Mab's in the later years of her life, she is devoted to celebrating the goodness of life with love, old-fashioned romance, and roses—"red ones, with lots of baby's breath and fern."

A Letter to Our Readers

Dear Reader:

Welcome to the world of Serenade Books—a series designed to bring you the most beautiful love stories in the world of inspirational romance. They will uplift you, encourage you, and provide hours of wholesome entertainment, so thousands of readers have testified. In order that we might better contribute to your reading enjoyment, we would appreciate your taking a few minutes to respond to the following questions and return to:

Editor, Serenade Books
The Zondervan Publishing House
1415 Lake Drive, S.E.
Grand Rapids, Michigan 49506

1. Did you enjoy reading A NEW LOVE?

☐ Very much. I would like to see more books by this author!
☐ Moderately
☐ I would have enjoyed it more if _____

_____

2. Where did you purchase this book? _____

3. What influenced your decision to purchase this book?

☐ Cover   ☐ Back cover copy
☐ Title   ☐ Friends
☐ Publicity   ☐ Other _____

4. What are some inspirational themes you would like to see treated in future books?

_____

5. Please indicate your age range:
   - ☐ Under 18   ☐ 25–34   ☐ 46–55
   - ☐ 18–24   ☐ 35–45   ☐ Over 55

6. If you are interested in receiving information about our Serenade Home Reader Service, in which you will be offered new and exciting novels on a regular basis, please give us your name and address. (This does NOT obligate you for membership.)

Name _____

Occupation _____

Address _____

City _____ State _____ Zip _____

Serenade / Saga books are inspirational romances in historical settings, designed to bring you a joyful, heart-lifting reading experience.

Serenade / Saga books available in your local book store:

#1 Summer Snow, Sandy Dengler
#2 Call Her Blessed, Jeanette Gilge
#3 Ina, Karen Baker Kletzing
#4 Juliana of Clover Hill, Brenda Knight Graham
#5 Song of the Nereids, Sandy Dengler
#6 Anna's Rocking Chair, Elaine Watson
#7 In Love's Own Time, Susan C. Feldhake
#8 Yankee Bride, Jane Peart
#9 Light of My Heart, Kathleen Karr
#10 Love Beyond Surrender, Susan C. Feldhake
#11 All the Days After Sunday, Jeannette Gilge
#12 Winterspring, Sandy Dengler
#13 Hand Me Down the Dawn,
     Mary Harwell Sayler
#14 Rebel Bride, Jane Peart
#15 Speak Softly, Love, Kathleen Yapp
#16 From This Day Forward, Kathleen Karr
#17 The River Between, Jacquelyn Cook
#18 Valiant Bride, Jane Peart
#19 Wait for the Sun, Maryn Langer
#20 Kincaid of Cripple Creek, Peggy Darty
#21 Love's Gentle Journey, Kay Cornelius
#22 Applegate Landing, Jean Conrad
#23 Beyond the Smoky Curtain,
     Mary Harwell Sayler
#24 To Dwell in the Land, Elaine Watson
#25 Moon for a Candle, Maryn Langer
#26 The Conviction of Charlotte Grey,
     Jeanne Cheyney
#27 Opal Fire, Sandy Dengler
#28 Divide the Joy, Maryn Langer

Serenade / Serenata books are inspirational romances in contemporary settings, designed to bring you a joyful, heart-lifting reading experience.

Serenade / Serenata books available in your local bookstore:

#1 On Wings of Love, Elaine L. Schulte
#2 Love's Sweet Promise, Susan C. Feldhake
#3 For Love Along, Susan C. Feldhake
#4 Love's Late Spring, Lydia Heermann
#5 In Comes Love, Mab Graff Hoover
#6 Fountain of Love, Velma S. Daniels and Peggy E. King.
#7 Morning Song, Linda Herring
#8 A Mountain to Stand Strong, Peggy Darty
#9 Love's Perfect Image, Judy Baer
#10 Smoky Mountain Sunrise, Yvonne Lehman
#11 Greengold Autumn, Donna Fletcher Crow
#12 Irresistible Love, Elaine Anne McAvoy
#13 Eternal Flame, Lurlene McDaniel
#14 Windsong, Linda Herring
#15 Forever Eden, Barbara Bennett
#16 Call of the Dove, Madge Harrah
#17 The Desires of Your Heart, Donna Fletcher Crow
#18 Tender Adversary, Judy Baer
#19 Halfway to Heaven, Nancy Johanson
#20 Hold Fast the Dream, Lurlene McDaniel
#21 The Disguise of Love, Mary LaPietra
#22 Through a Glass Darkly, Sara Mitchell
#23 More Than a Summer's Love, Yvonne Lehman
#24 Language of the Heart, Jeanne Anders
#25 One More River, Suzanne Pierson Ellison
#26 Journey Toward Tomorrow, Karyn Carr
#27 Flower of the Sea, Amanda Clark
#28 Shadows Along the Ice, Judy Baer
#29 Born to Be One, Cathie LeNoir

#30 Heart Aflame, Susan Kirby
#31 By Love Restored, Nancy Johanson
#32 Karaleen, Mary Carpenter Reid
#33 Love's Full Circle, Lurlene McDaniel
#34 A New Love, Mab Graff Hoover
#35 The Lessons of Love, Susan Phillips
#36 For Always, Molly Noble Bull

Watch for other books in both the *Serenade/Saga* (historical) and *Serenade/Serenata* (contemporary) series coming soon.